A CURATOR'S QUEST

GOING

FOR THE

GOLD

DAVID B. WARREN

RIVER GROVE
BOOKS

Published by River Grove Books
Austin, TX
www.rivergrovebooks.com

Distributed by River Grove Books

Design and composition by Greenleaf Book Group
Cover design by Greenleaf Book Group
Cover images used under license from ©Adobestock.com

Publisher's Cataloging-in-Publication data is available.

Print ISBN: 978-1-63299-980-1

eBook ISBN: 978-1-63299-981-8

First Edition

*In loving memory of my wife, Janie,
who introduced me to Umbria.*

AUTHOR'S NOTE

This story is fiction that comes from my imagination and also experiences during the forty summers I spent in Umbria. All the characters are also fictitious—some amalgams of people I have known with details rearranged, as are some of the events described. I have taken liberty with a few historical facts. Oliver De Lancey (sic), who did marry Phila Franks, was the brother of James De Lancey. So, Oliver and Phila were not direct ancestors of this story's Delancys. James De Lancey was Lt. Governor of New York, but the Bahamas governorship is fiction. A pair of silver, trumpet-shaped candlesticks made by Daniel Christian Fueter are at Winterthur. Fueter was one of the few American colonial-era smiths who made small objects in gold. A Fueter gold whistle and bells—an eighteenth-century infant's toy—is in the Garvan Collection. Colonial American gold hollow ware, as described herein, is, however, pure fiction. A New York Chippendale-style desk-and-bookcase attributed to Henry Hardcastle is in the Chipstone Collection. I am aware that the milieu in which this story takes place represents a small, elite slice of society as a whole, during the early 1980s, and for that I make no apologies.

The idyllic and bucolic Italy of rural Umbria, as experienced by Dickie in the summer of 1980, was in fact a far cry from the terrorist-dominated and dangerous world that was Italy in the decade of the 1970s and early 1980s. Most prominent among the far-left terrorist organizations was one called *le Brigate Rosse*, or Red Brigades. This guerilla group, modeled on Latin American movements, as well as the Italian partisan movement of World War II, was responsible for numerous violent incidents, including kidnapping and murder of prominent businessmen, politicians, and judges. The most notorious was the kidnapping and subsequent murder of former Prime Minister Aldo Moro in 1978. As a result, wealthy and prominent Italians, who lived in constant fear, adjusted their way of life accordingly. Rich men no longer drove around in large expensive chauffeured cars—Lancias, Mercedes, BMWs—but rather stealthily traveled with their chauffeur in tiny Fiat Cinquecentos. Ladies no longer wore expensive gemstones, or even real gold, when going out, but rather left those things in their personal safes and wore only costume jewelry. While Dickie's hosts, the di Florianos, did not mention it to him, the long reach of the Red Brigades extended even into their neighborhood. Several local absentee owners, upon return to their summer villas, found that they had been invaded by Red Brigaders and totally stripped of everything of value. The local populace, while too afraid of reprisal to stop such raids, did after the fact report to the owners who was responsible.

1

UMBRIA, ITALY

July 1980

Dickie settled down in his business-class seat on board TWA flight 880, bound from JFK to Rome, and felt a wave of stress begin to peel away. There had been two frantic days at the Museum getting all his affairs in order before being able to leave for a much-anticipated vacation in Umbria. And prior to that, the difficult months before the divorce from his estranged wife became final. Dickie was indeed ready for a break.

A tall, slim man of athletic build, with curly blond hair and deep blue eyes, Dickie, as he was known to all, was Richard Boudinot Stockton Read, Curator of Metalwares in the American Decorative Arts department at New York's renowned City Art Museum.

Born in Philadelphia in 1940, Dickie, an only child, grew up in New Castle, Delaware, living in a late Georgian house on The Strand, surrounded by objects from his family's colonial past. His parents, Elizabeth Busby Darnell and George Gray Read, were proud of their pre-Revolutionary heritage. Each was descended from a signer of the Declaration of Independence—she, of Burlington County, New Jersey Quaker stock, and a descendant of Richard Stockton; he a descendant of George Read and a member of an old and distinguished Delaware family of lawyers. In the nineteenth century, Elizabeth's family, the Darnells, had become wealthy through ownership in several Atlantic City hotels. George Read, an attorney, was Senior Partner of a large Wilmington law firm.

Educated at Wilmington Friends School and graduating from The Hill School in nearby Pottstown, Pennsylvania, Dickie attended Yale University, majoring in English. One of his elective courses was devoted to the history of American decorative arts. The course, fondly known as "Pots and Pans," was a favorite of Yale athletes, as the professor guaranteed a passing grade to any jock who enrolled. While he had grown up surrounded by colonial Americana, he had never taken any interest in it. Dickie, who rowed on the Yale 150-pound crew, initially enrolled simply to get an easy A, but as the semester progressed, he became increasingly fascinated as he learned in depth about colonial furniture and silver.

While he had always thought he would follow his family's tradition and study law, the attraction of possibly working at a museum with American decorative arts persuaded him to opt for another course in the subject. Although he knew that museum work would never be lucrative, the generous trust funds set up for him by his Darnell grandparents would, income-wise, provide a comfortable cushion. The logical graduate-level school for a career in American decorative arts was the Winterthur Program in Early American Culture at the University of Delaware. Dickie was initially reluctant to consider applying because, as an Ivy League Yalie, he looked down on the University of Delaware as a lesser place of education, and then, it also was in his home turf. However, upon further thought, he realized the quality of the collection at the Winterthur Museum was superb, and as the major component of the program, its excellence mitigated his feelings about Delaware. His application was accepted near the end of his senior year, and in the late summer after his Yale graduation, he formally entered the two-year program. The two years sped by, and, in March of his second year, his thesis on Wilmington, Delaware, silversmith Bancroft Woodcock was formally accepted. Upon graduation, Dickie joined the staff at New York's City Art Museum as an Insley Blair Fellow. This led to his being hired as a curatorial assistant in the American Department. He subsequently rose through the ranks to his current position as a full curator responsible for metalware—silver and pewter.

Mid-July of 1980 found Dickie on his way to stay as a guest of his friend Arabella di Floriano, an American-born conservator at the Museum, who was married to an aristocratic Italian, Il Marchese Luca Rossi di Floriano. The visit would be based at the sprawling summer country house of Luca's mother and siblings, located above the Tiber near Camerata, a *frazione* of Todi, in the Umbrian province of Perugia. The stone house, built over centuries, was anchored in the center by a tall medieval watchtower.

Arabella, slim and short of stature, wore her blonde hair pulled back into a short but elegant ponytail. A native of Vermont, she had met Luca while studying painting conservation in Rome. Luca, tall and broad-shouldered with dark, nearly black hair, was the scion of a noble Modenese family that had migrated to Rome. After their marriage, the di Florianos moved to New York, where Arabella was employed as a paintings conservator at the City Art Museum. Luca became successful in investment banking.

Following the overnight flight and early morning arrival at Rome's Fumicino, Dickie was met by a driver sent by his hosts, and whisked along the Autostrada del Sole, from Rome to Umbria and the villa of the di Florianos, arriving just before lunch. Arabella and Luca met him at the front door.

"*Ben venuto*, Dickie," said Arabella as Dickie kissed her on both cheeks in the European manner.

Luca, also in the European manner, embraced Dickie, saying, "May I add my words of welcome to Umbria and our house?"

Dickie was then ushered inside to the *salone*, which had a soaring ceiling supported by a massive truss and beam system. Floor to ceiling French doors gave access to the expansive covered portico overlooking the Tiber.

"We are having lunch here," explained Arabella, escorting Dickie outside. The three sat down to a leisurely repast of pasta and salad, washed down with glasses of *Torre di Gianno*, a local white wine from nearby Torgiano. During lunch, Dickie mentioned that just before leaving New York, his mother told him that he had a cousin by marriage who lived in the Todi area.

"Oh, who is that?" asked Arabella.

"She is called Sara Orsini. Do you know her?"

"Oh yes," was the response. "They live across the Tiber from us, but they are not here now as they summer in Normandy."

"The Orsinis were old friends of my family in Rome," added Luca, "and they moved up here around the same time as my parents acquired this property."

At the end of the meal, Dickie took leave of his hosts. As he prepared for a jet lag–inspired nap, he mused to himself, "Too bad I won't meet my Italian cousin."

Late in the afternoon, while feeling rested and refreshed, Dickie decided that a short run would get his circulation going. He set out from the villa, up an unpaved road, called by the Italians "*una strada bianca*," or "a white road," toward the village of Camerata. At the top of the hill, the road became paved and led him down toward the village. The main part of the ancient village was densely built on a high promontory. The more recent, paved road circled around its base. As he jogged by, he caught sight, in a wheat field below and to his right, of a small peak-roofed stone structure with a rounded apse on the end wall. It looked to him like it was very old and maybe Romanesque. That it was isolated, all alone out in a wheat field, added an air of mystery. Somehow it seemed much older than Camerata. Dickie was curious to know its history.

In the early evening, Arabella, Luca, and Dickie met for *aperitivi* on the portico.

"How was your afternoon?" asked Arabella.

"It was terrific," Dickie replied, plucking an olive from a small glass bowl. "I went on a jog and saw what looked like the most interesting little church, maybe a chapel, in the wheat field below Camerata. Can you tell me anything about it?"

"Luca," said Arabella, turning to her husband, "you are our local authority. What can you tell Dickie about it?"

"Well," responded the Marchese, "yes, I know it. It is late medieval, Romanesque, and is one of the little devotional chapels built around here in the twelve hundreds. It is owned by the Church, but is actually on the property of our cook, Isalina Morretini. It really is quite charming. It has some nice, old, though much-faded, frescos painted by an unknown artist, but clearly in the Todi style. If you are interested, I am sure she would be glad to open the chapel for you."

"Wow," responded Dickie, "that would be fabulous. Can you set that up?"

"Arabella," said Luca, "why don't you ask Isalina to come out for a moment so we can ask her about it?"

"*Subito,*" replied Arabella and headed off in the direction of the kitchen. While she was gone, Luca explained that Isalina, fortunately, spoke fairly good English. A few minutes later, Arabella returned, accompanied by a diminutive middle-aged woman with delicate facial features and ginger-colored hair. Luca explained to her that Dickie had seen the church from afar and wondered if he might be able to go inside.

"Yes," Isalina told Dickie, "we take care of the little church. My family are keepers of the key, so I would be glad to take you there. Do you know when you would like to see it?"

"Would tomorrow be too soon for you?" Dickie replied.

"No, that would be fine. What time would be convenient for you?" she asked.

"I think ten would be good," was his answer.

"*Va bene*," replied Isalina. "Please come first to my house and then we can walk over to the church together."

After a superb dinner of *gnocchi verde*, grilled *trotta salmone* from Lake Trasimeno, and fresh green beans from the *orto*, or vegetable garden, all finished off with a traditional pastry, *torta di nonna*, again accompanied with much wine, Dickie, excited about tomorrow but deliciously fatigued, retired to his room, and almost instantly was lulled to sleep by the gentle, cool night air that wafted in through the open windows.

The next morning, Dickie arose early and, after a swim in the pool located on the terrace level below the portico, he met the di Florianos up on the portico, where they breakfasted on sliced peaches, *Pecorino Toscana* cheese, and bread fresh from the local bakery.

"The bread," Arabella told Dickie, tearing off a piece, "is baked in a wood-fueled oven. It's made without salt in the traditional Umbrian manner. Before the unification of Italy, Umbria was part of the Papal States. This way of baking bread dates from medieval times—the Umbrians found a way to avoid a Papal tax on salt," she explained.

"Thanks for the explanation. Mm, this bread," mumbled Dickie as he munched on a large piece, "is fantastic."

The repast was completed with hot strong coffee served in individual little Bialetti espresso brewing pots, the type found all over Italy. As they ate, Luca outlined to Dickie how to get to Isalina's house. "Go up the hill toward Camerata, but bear right on the road to Amelia. This will curve around the valley below Camerata, and after you pass through a *bosco*, a small woods, you will see a *strada bianca* on your left and a sign, *La Foca*. That road will take you to Isalina's house. You can use the Cinquecento, which we keep on hand for local errands."

Just before ten, Dickie got into the tiny Fiat Cinquecento. As he started it up, he realized he had forgotten the challenge, but also fun, of driving a stick-shift car. He arrived at the *La Foca* turnoff a few minutes later, and descended down the hill to the end of the road, where a large stone farmhouse stood. As he parked the car next to the house, Isalina came out the front door to greet him. "*Buon giorno*, Signore Dickie. I am happy that you came. Let's walk over to the church," she said as she gestured to a grassy path on her left that ran through the field of tall golden wheat. The path led to the rear, semi-circular apse side of the tile-roofed chapel. They proceeded around to the severely plain front façade. Above the central doorway was a large square window, the main source of light for the dim interior. While the exterior was built of random fieldstone, the interior, in contrast, was finished with carefully cut ashlar blocks. Directly ahead was the interior of the apse. In the arched space was a freestanding stone altar, supported by a cylindrical stone shaft raised on a small dais. On the apsidal wall behind the altar were the faded remnants of a fresco that depicted a haloed figure seated inside an apse. *Probably the patron saint of the chapel,* Dickie thought. On the wall to the right were several more remnants of fresco depicting standing haloed male figures.

As if reading his mind, Isalina said, "That is San Silvestro, the patron saint of this church."

After looking around, Dickie's eyes suddenly focused on the altar. What caught his attention was a pair of silver candlesticks—not just ordinary candlesticks, but sticks made in the form of an inverted trumpet. Dickie knew, from a recent visit to Switzerland, that this form was uniquely Swiss and dated from the mid-eighteenth century. *How on earth,* he wondered, *would Swiss candlesticks end up in this remote little chapel?*

"At my museum in America," Dickie said to Isalina, "old silver is my specialty. Those candlesticks look very interesting— would it be all right if I examined them?"

"Of course," replied Isalina, with a smile. "I am glad you like them. They were a gift in honor of the lost girl."

At the moment, more interested in the silver than a lost girl, Dickie mumbled, "Okay, thank you," as he stepped closer to the altar and reached for one of the candlesticks. He removed the candle and picked up the stick to take a closer look for any clues as to its origin. To his amazement, located on the upper edge of the socket, he saw the mark "DCF" stamped within an oval and below that, "N: York." With typical curatorial curiosity, he then upended the stick to see if there was any further information and, lo and behold, there was an engraving in script. "The gift of ASD van W 1947," it read. The other stick was similarly marked. He noticed, too, that there was a coat of arms—a shield with three crescents—engraved on the trumpet-shaped base. Dickie knew from examples in his collection at the City Art Museum, that DCF was the touchmark of the Swiss-born silversmith Daniel Christian Fueter, who worked in New York City in the mid-eighteenth century. Fueter's Swiss background would explain the choice of the trumpet-shaped form, but not how his work got to Umbria. The notation "N: York" confirmed an American, and not Swiss, origin. But who was ASD van W, and why 1947? He was stunned by this discovery.

"I wonder," he asked Isalina, "do you know who the lost girl was and how she is related to the history of these candlesticks?"

"I am not exactly sure of the details of where the candlesticks came from," replied Isalina, "but I do know they are somehow connected with a child who around here is referred to as 'the lost girl.' My great-uncle, Padre Giovanni Ricci, the priest in Camerata, and responsible for this church, was somehow involved. He and the girl were both executed by German soldiers who were occupying the area in 1944. I don't know a lot more about it, as it happened before I was born, but I have two older cousins, Euphemia and Silena Ricci, who were young girls at that time. They are sort of our local resource for Camerata's history. If you would like, we could call them and ask if they would meet with you."

"That would be terrific," Dickie said, nodding.

"Their English is difficult to understand, because of their heavy local accent," Isalina added, "but perhaps the Marchesa Arabella would be able to go with you. Maybe we can talk further when I come to the villa this evening to prepare dinner."

"I would like that very much," Dickie said.

That evening, the di Florianos had a *festa*, a dinner party, in Dickie's honor. As Dickie spoke limited Italian, the guests were all English-speaking Italians or Americans who either lived or summered in the area. The guest list included a Roman prince with his Australian wife, a Hollywood film star and his German wife, and a prominent New York gallery owner, who, with his wife, a retired German TV star, summered at Bel Forte, their nearby medieval castle. Also included were Caroline Kuchler, longtime Paris correspondent for the New York–based magazine *The Knickerbocker*, and her husband, Victor, an anthropologist; Ramona Warner, a well-known

American sculptor, and her husband, Carter Bel Warner, a retired journalist; and the Marchesa Lucrezia Bianchini Atti. The Marchesa, an elegant lady of about forty, with reddish-brown hair and dark, nearly black eyes, lived in a nearby castle, Crispiano, which she had inherited from her Florentine grandparents, Il Principe and La Principessa Chiravalle. In the course of the spirited dinner table conversation, which covered a wide range of topics and ran from politics to art world gossip, Dickie mentioned his visit to the little church, that he was told about a lost girl, and his discovery of a pair of colonial American silver candlesticks.

"In the next day or so, I have a pending visit with two older local ladies, the Ricci sisters," Dickie continued, "who are related to a priest killed by the Germans. My hope is to learn something from them about the pair of American eighteenth-century silver candlesticks that are on the altar in the church," he told the party. "Also, maybe they can tell me more about the lost girl."

"We've all heard about the legend of a lost girl, but nobody seems to know the details," Carter Warner said. "You might want to talk to the current Camerata priest, Padre Francesco Pianigianni—he might have some pertinent documents in his archive. I'd be happy to make the introduction."

Lucrezia Atti mentioned that the Ricci sisters were not only the nieces of the assassinated Padre Giovanni, but also the daughters of Michele Ricci, who for many years had been the steward of her grandparents' two local castles, Crispiano and Mariano. "I remember hearing that Michele was somehow involved with the girl," Lucrezia said. "I was told that both Michele's brother, Padre Giovanni Ricci, and the American girl were executed by the Nazis during the war. But I'm not sure of the details."

"That's such a terrible story," said Dickie, "but it piques my curiosity to learn more about the whole saga of the poor lost girl, whoever she was."

Because of all the work involved in getting ready for the *festa*, neither Isalina nor Arabella had time to discuss a visit to the Ricci sisters, and Dickie realized that might have to wait a day or two. However, Carter Warner surprised him with a phone call at mid-morning the next day—he was calling to relate he had been in touch with Padre Francesco. Unfortunately, the Padre had to be in Perugia that day, but would be happy to receive Dickie the following morning. "The Padre suggested you come to the Camerata church at ten tomorrow," Warner told Dickie. "I hope that works with your schedule."

"Thank you so much," replied Dickie. "My schedule here is delightfully open! So, I will be there then."

"Good," said Warner. "The village is so small you can't get lost—just look out for the crenellated tower of the church. The Padre will meet you at the front entrance."

With no appointment until the following morning, Dickie spent the rest of the day at leisure, soaking up the sun by the pool.

The next morning, Dickie opted to walk, rather than drive, up to Camerata. Taking the same road he had jogged on, he walked along the edge of the village. He came upon the local grocery store and bar, and, as he looked up the narrow, cobblestone-paved lane that led up into the central area, he caught sight of the stone church's crenellated tower. He ascended up the steep hill to the level of the church. When he arrived at the front steps leading up to the central door, the door swung open before he had a chance to knock, and Dickie was greeted by a bald, slightly portly, middle-aged man wearing the long black garb of a priest.

"*Buon giorno, signore! Sono Padre Francesco,*" said the priest. "*Mi scusi,* but I do not speak well English, but I will try."

"*Va bene,*" replied Dickie, "I will try to use my poor Italian."

Smiling, Padre Francesco gestured toward the door and said, "Please come with me to my *ufficio* and counsel me on what you wish to know. Signore Warner said to me that it was about the lost girl. I do not know much. It's the Ricci family who can tell you all about her, but there is a letter here that might be of interest to you."

They passed through the dim church and on to the sacristy at the rear left, where the Padre had a little office. On one wall was a series of shelves loaded with fat gray manila binders, each secured with black ribbon. Padre Francesco reached up and brought down one, which, he noted, had documents for

1947. Opening up the binder, he leafed through the voluminous array of papers, and then extracted an envelope. "*Ecco*," he grunted, "this is what I was looking for." He opened the envelope, pulled out its contents, unfolded the letter, and passed it to Dickie. "I think this will help explain to you about the silver candlesticks," he said.

The letterhead bore the name and address of Flanigan and Caldwell at 120 Broadway, New York, 4, NY. Dickie was familiar with this eminent New York firm, as his father had often worked with them.

New York November 27, 1947

Gentlemen,
At the direction of our client, Mrs. Adelaide S. D. van Wyck, we are herewith sending you a pair of antique silver candlesticks for use in the church where her niece, Alexandra, was offered refuge during the Nazi German occupation of Camerata, Italy in 1944. They are sent with Mrs. van Wyck's grateful thanks for perilous risks taken by your priest and the kindness shown her niece by the citizens of Camerata.

Dickie thanked the Padre for sharing this information with him, remarking that it was both very interesting and very helpful.

Well, thought Dickie as he returned to the villa, *that explains how the eighteenth-century New York silver candlesticks got here and the meaning of the inscription "the gift of ASD van W" and "1947." But who is, or was, Mrs. van Wyck? At least I know she was the aunt of the lost girl and that the girl's name was Alexandra, so that's certainly a start.* The idea of colonial-period silver from New York piqued Dickie's interest. He mused, with typical curatorial acquisitiveness, *van Wyck is an old New York name. I bet my director, Alicia Milhaus, with her decades of experience, will know exactly who Adelaide van Wyck is. And maybe there is more early silver in her family!*

Private telephone service was relatively new to the rural villages surrounding Todi, and the Ricci sisters' phone had only been installed the previous spring. "Often, when I try to call them, I get no answer," Arabella explained to Dickie. "I once asked Silena about that, and she said since she didn't know who was calling, she wasn't sure she wanted to speak with them."

Dickie laughed. "Makes sense—I don't like answering the phone either."

That day, as it turned out, the Ricci sisters, who did not have a car and liked to hop a ride into Todi whenever they could cadge one, were, for once, actually not home. So, when Arabella tried to ring them to arrange Dickie's visit, she had gotten no answer. It wasn't until the next day that she tried again, was able to make contact, and a meeting was set up for eleven the following morning. That was the next to last day of Dickie's stay with the di Florianos before his return flight would take him back to New York.

The Ricci sisters lived in a *borgo*, a communal gathering of homes, perched on the hilltop across the valley from the di Floriano villa. Called Olmeda, the *borgo* overlooked the little church next to Isalina's house. The large, three-story, square, stone structure was of interminable age, probably much of it medieval, and tradition held that it was on the site of a Roman fortification of the Severan Period. Access from the road was through an arched doorway that led into an open lateral street, likely a remnant of an interior court. On either side, the space had been converted into small individual homes, most of which were inhabited by the extended Ricci clan. Arabella and Dickie parked outside the arched doorway of the *borgo* and walked in.

The Ricci sisters were at their front door, eagerly awaiting their arrival. For them, Arabella had explained in advance, life was a bit humdrum, so the visit and the opportunity to talk about the town's history was an exciting event. They entered the sisters' home through a narrow passage whose white plastered walls were punctuated by doorways of warm brown chestnut; the floor was a buff-colored terracotta. They were ushered to the right into a little *salotto*, or parlor, furnished with overstuffed, plush, velour-covered furniture. After everyone was seated, Euphemia, the older sister, asked if they would like a coffee, and as the answer was yes, she hustled off to the kitchen and soon returned with a tray of tiny cups filled with thick dark espresso.

After initial polite chitchat, Arabella explained why they were there. The sisters began to recount their tale. The two could not have been more different in appearance— Euphemia, tall, thin, with a long gaunt face; Silena, small, plump, with a pudgy, snub-nosed face. But when they spoke, they started and ended each other's sentences. They were avid to begin, and their words spilled out rapidly. As they spoke, their broken English was heavily nuanced by the local Italian accent, which made the words sound like they were growling. Often it was impossible for Dickie to follow. At those times, Arabella would step in with a translation. Their fascinating story unfolded during the following hour.

The Florentine Chiravalle family, the sisters related, owned many properties in Umbria. Two of them were castles near Camerata—Crispiano and Mariano.

"Our Papa," Euphemia said, "who was called Michele, was the Prince Chiravalle's local steward. He had the important position of being responsible for everything to do with the two castles and their staffs. In the early spring of 1944," she continued, "Papa received a message from the Princess Chiravalle that he should be on the lookout for two valuable shipments, sent down to Umbria from Florence."

"He was told that one," Silena interrupted, "would arrive accompanied by Dottore Piero Galeassi-Lisi. The *dottore*," she explained, "was not only a Chiravalle family friend, but also served as the personal physician to Pope Pius. Our family," Silena said proudly, "also knew the *dottore*, because he had a summer house not far from Camerata, near the village of Fiore."

"Papa was told," Euphemia interjected, "that the other shipment would arrive by truck."

Silena continued, "Several days later, Papa was alerted that the truck shipment would arrive the next night. We never knew exactly what was in it, but we did know that it came in the dark of night and was something very valuable that needed to be hidden from the Germans. We had been told that in Florence, like here in Todi, the Germans had taken total control over that city."

"Papa," said Euphemia, "never explained, other than that the shipment was safely hidden in one of the castles. After the war, Silena and I heard that the shipment was the Chiravalles' collection of paintings. We remember when they were later taken out of Il Castello di Mariano here in Umbria and returned to the Palazzo Chiravalle in Florence."

"The second shipment," said Silena, "turned out to be a young girl who arrived in the company of Doctor Galeassi-Lisi. As the personal doctor of the Pope, he was able to travel more freely than the rest of us Italians. Our movements fell totally under the scrutiny of the German army after our country withdrew from the war in September of 1943."

"We later learned," said Euphemia, "the doctor traveled by rail from Florence to Orvieto, accompanied by a young girl, identified to the authorities as his ward. He was met, not by a car, as the Germans had prohibited private vehicles, but by a horse and buggy. The journey through the mountainous landscape in the valley beside the Tiber took nearly a full day."

"Papa met them when they finally arrived at the doctor's villa in Fiore," continued Euphemia. "The doctor explained to Papa that, as the girl was in danger, it was the princess's wish that he as her trusted steward take the girl into his care and hide her presence from the authorities. We knew almost nothing about her."

"Only that her name was Alexandra," added Silena, "and that she was in danger from the Nazis, as she had Jewish blood."

"Below Olmeda, but on our property," Silana continued, "we owned an old stone farmhouse. It had been long abandoned and was tumbledown. By the wartime, there were sheep stabled in the ground floor. Papa decided that was the perfect place to hide the girl. He realized the second-floor room was still somewhat habitable, and that was where he decided to hide her."

"Papa knew," interjected Euphemia, "it was not possible to heat the room with the fireplace, because the smoke would show someone was living there, but heat rising from the sheep, stabled below on the ground floor, would help some."

"Papa gave Euphemia and me the daily job of bringing down food and water," said Silena.

The sisters related that all went well for some weeks, until one fateful day when German troops who were occupying Todi came to the area to take a census of the local inhabitants.

"Unfortunately," said Euphemia, "I was carrying an empty food basket and another filled with the girl's laundry, when I was stopped by two German soldiers as I came up the hill from the hiding house. The Germans demanded to know where I was coming from and what was the meaning of my baskets. I was so scared I could barely speak, and the Germans did not understand my Italian. That made them very angry, so I was arrested right there, hustled up to the village, and taken to the church, where they continued to ask questions. Papa, who was at home, saw that I had been caught while coming from the hiding house, and knew that soon the Germans would search through it. He did not want to leave the girl unprotected, so he sent urgent word to his brother, my *Zio*, Padre Giovanni. Immediately understanding the danger, *Zio* hurried down from Camerata to the ruined house and hustled the girl over to the little ancient church that was located in the wheat field near the hiding house," she said.

Silena picked up the narrative. "We later learned that the German soldiers, while in Camerata, received word from Todi that, on the previous night, a band of young local men had changed all the road signs in the area, so that the road to Asproli became to Morre, Izzalini to Aqua Loreto, and so forth. What was worse, however, from their point of view, was the news that the same night, a band from the resistance had managed to blow up the bridge that crossed the Tiber below Todi at Ponte Cuti. We were told that the outraged German commander in Todi sent word to Camerata that the troops must immediately return to Todi and assist in interrogation of the locals. Before they left, however, the soldiers in Camerata, infuriated by the changed road signs and the news of the sabotage, ordered that all the area citizens should be rounded up and herded into the town's church for questioning. They learned that my absent *Zio* was down in the little church, and when they went there to return him to the village, they discovered he was hiding the young girl. Clearly, in their minds, he was involved in something nefarious, and they ordered him to come with them. *Zio* mistakenly tried to take sanctuary in the church. His resistance to the Germans' commands further infuriated them, and they shot him and the girl on the spot."

"So," said the Ricci sisters in unison, "that is the story of the lost girl."

"Good heavens," said Dickie as he and Arabella rose to leave, "what a dreadful story, and so sad too. Thank you for sharing it with me."

That evening, Dickie's last at the di Floriano villa, they were invited across the Naia valley to have dinner with Lucrezia Atti at Il Castello di Crispiano. As they approached the village of Crispiano, the castle rose like a large stone block against the horizon. Luca drove their ancient Lancia through the postern gate and parked at the bottom of the main castle wall.

At that moment, Lucrezia appeared in the large arched entrance, which gave access to a grand stone staircase leading up to the second floor of the castle interior. Wearing a colorful, chic Pucci-designed summer dress, she descended down the final few staircase steps.

"Welcome to Crispiano," she said, speaking in a lilting musical tone mixed with the posh accent of the English upper class. "Dickie, I am so glad you came—and it's always a joy to have you here, Arabella and Luca. It's a lovely night," she continued, "so we will have *aperitivi* al fresco on the terrace," she said, as she gestured to her left. "Dickie," she went on with a slightly mischievous smile, "I trust you like prosecco, our Italian bubbly, no?"

They settled down for prosecco on the wide stone terrace, overlooking the valley. To his mild surprise, Dickie noticed that Lucrezia, dark-reddish-haired and of dark complexion, had a very becoming figure, slim waisted but at the same time curvaceous. As she spoke her narrative was accompanied by animated gestures, and her spontaneous smile was like a ray of sunshine. *Maybe I am getting over the divorce thing*, he thought. He couldn't help but feel a little pleased when Luca and Arabella decided that before dinner they would like to go and see the newly landscaped garden Lucrezia had just completed on the other side of the castle.

He was left alone with her, and Lucrezia began to explain that the castle dated from the thirteenth century. In the sixteenth century, it had been given by the Pope to an earlier Prince Chiravalle, as a reward for his services in a war against the Holy Roman Emperor.

"My grandfather," Lucrezia said, "left the castle to my mother when he died in 1950 as part of a program of dividing his Umbrian properties between his children. My Uncle Carlo received the ancestral seat, Castello Mariano, and my Aunt Anna Maria, the Titignano property near Orvieto. My mother gave Crispiano to me."

"Wow," said Dickie with a smile, "you sure were lucky. I've not seen much yet, but it certainly seems like a good deal to me."

"I've been talking too much about myself and my family," Lucrezia said with a grin. "Dickie, tell me how you are enjoying your stay in our beloved Umbria—we Italians call it the green heart of Italy. And what have you been up to since our dinner the other night? Keeping out of trouble I hope!" she teased.

"Absolutely, I am sad to say," Dickie replied. "But seriously, in the hope of finding out more about the lost girl, Arabella arranged a most interesting visit with those two elderly women, the sisters named Ricci, who told me there were two mysterious wartime shipments from Florence to Umbria by the then-Princess Chiravalle. One was the girl with the Pope's doctor, but they did not know much about the other."

"Well," Lucrezia responded with a smile, "that Princess Chiravalle was my grandmother. You now know about the shipment with the doctor, but I can tell you more about the other mysterious shipment."

"I would very much like that," Dickie replied.

"Well," Lucrezia began, setting her glass of prosecco on the table and looking intently at Dickie, "in early 1944, the situation in Florence became more difficult. The Germans took complete control of the city and began to acquire works of art from Florentines who came under their suspicions for one reason or another. My grandmother feared for the famed collection of Renaissance and Baroque paintings that were housed in the Palazzo Chiravalle—you may know it, it's the huge buff-colored complex overlooking the Arno."

"Oh," Dickie said, nodding. "I remember seeing it from across the river, but I never knew what it was."

"Yes." Lucrezia smiled. "So, my grandmother and her staff updated the palace's inventory, and marked the back of each work of art in blue paint with the family coat of arms. The paintings were then secretly loaded into a large, covered lorry that was parked in the interior courtyard of the palace. In the dark of night, it was time to leave for the trip down to Umbria, where the paintings would be hidden at a family property."

Lucrezia then explained how the servants, knowing that if they were caught they would probably be shot by the Germans, were too afraid to undertake the drive.

"They simply refused?" said Dickie. "Though I can't say that I blame them."

"They did. So, my grandmother," Lucrezia explained, "replied, 'Well, I will drive the lorry myself,' and so she did. The paintings were taken to the Castello Mariano near Camerata, where my grandmother was met by her faithful steward, Michele Ricci. He and his staff transferred the pictures down into the lower interstices of the ancient castle, where they were carefully stowed in a series of secret rooms. The entrance was then carefully sealed up."

"Later," Lucrezia said, "when the Germans went on their rampage, following the bombing of the Ponte Cuti bridge, they stormed into the castle and searched through it from parapets to basement. They found nothing and no one hiding, but one overzealous soldier who decided to go deeper noticed a sealed doorway in the lowest area and managed to break it down. When he looked in, he saw a face shrouded in the gloomy light. In fear, he took a shot and then ran away. What is funny," laughed Lucrezia, "is that what he saw was a painting of Sant' Ilario, who happens to be the patron saint of our family. Later, my grandmother always told us how, when she left Sant' Ilario at the front of the stored paintings, she told him that she had done all that she could, and now it was up to him to protect the family treasure—and he did. If you look today at the Sant' Ilario, which hangs in the Palazzo's picture gallery, you can see the bullet hole in the top left corner."

"Wow," exclaimed Dickie, "what a fascinating story! Clearly your very brave grandmother was taking simultaneous protective steps against German atrocities—safeguarding her paintings, or in the case of the girl, who I am told was part Jewish, hiding her from arrest and a concentration camp. Do you know who the girl was and why your grandmother became involved?"

"No," replied Lucrezia, "that part of the story was never discussed with me. But my grandmother kept very meticulous records. At her death in 1947, all her papers were deposited in family archives at the Palazzo Chiravalle in Florence. So the answer might lie there."

Luca and Arabella returned from their garden visit, and the party moved inside to a large stone vaulted hall and settled into their multi-course dinner—ravioli stuffed with ricotta, grilled chicken, rabbit and sausage, *ciccoria* and broccoli, and finished off with a *misto* of gelatos. "The white wine, *San Sebastiano*," Lucrezia explained, "comes from one of our Chiravalle family vineyards overlooking the Tiber near Orvieto." After coffee and grappa, the di Florianos and Dickie took their leave, though Dickie felt reluctance to part with his attractive hostess. He thanked Lucrezia for her hospitality and the information about her grandmother. "Maybe someday, I will get to Florence and find out who the lost girl really was," he told her. *And I will probably never see this lady again*, Dickie mused to himself.

The next morning, right after breakfasting with Arabella and Luca, Dickie expressed to them heartfelt thanks for a wonderful week in their idyllic setting and then bade them farewell. Their car and driver sped him on the reverse of the previous week's trip, down the *autostrada* and on to Fumicino, where he caught his late morning TWA flight back to New York.

2

MANHATTAN

July 1980

Having cleared passport control and negotiated baggage claim, Dickie emerged from TWA's Saarinen terminal and located his ride into Manhattan, a beat-up old Buick provided by Tel Aviv Town Car, an "*el cheapo grande*" car service that Dickie had found through his younger, less well-heeled friends at the Museum. Not glamorous, but it sure beat a cab and the price was almost the same. The car delivered him to a Beaux Arts-vintage limestone townhouse located at mid-block on a tree-lined street between Madison and Fifth Avenue on the Upper East Side.

The apartment, the top floor of the town house—with windows on three sides—was a *pied-a-terre* for his parents when not in Delaware or their summer house in Boothbay Harbor, Maine. Dickie had moved there temporarily after he became homeless when, during the divorce process, it was no longer feasible or bearable to share an abode with his then-wife. And then, in the divorce, she was awarded their apartment at 91st and Park. His return to New York now brought it all back.

His former wife, Margaret Dorsey Bradford, was a fellow Wilmingtonian, some five years younger than Dickie. He had not known her when growing up, but when back in Wilmington as a Winterthur Fellow and an eligible bachelor, his was a frequent name on the guest lists for the debutante circuit. It was there he met Margaret at a tea dance. They dated off and on for a year until Dickie, having become sure he was in love, proposed. She said no, and they split, only to have her renew the relationship some months later. After two more splits and reunions, each generated by Margaret, they eventually married and then moved to New York when Dickie began his new job at the City Art Museum. They settled in a small second-floor apartment at the corner of 91st Street and Park Avenue. While their pre-marital sex was passionate, after marriage, things cooled hugely and then virtually ceased. The problem became clear when Margaret announced she had been having an affair with a woman friend and wanted out of the marriage.

Standing in front of his parents' townhouse, Dickie stared up at the elegant windows, recalling how crushed he had been. But he was lucky, too—for his mental health, he had both his work at the Museum and his Museum colleagues. He threw himself into his work and spent long hours at the office.

The week in Umbria had been a wonderful respite, and Dickie returned eager to pursue the quest to see if there were colonial silver treasures in the van Wyck family—potential acquisitions for his collection. But first he needed to find out who they were. On Monday morning, he called Museum Director Alicia Connally Milhaus, and asked if he could drop in for a brief chat and some advice. Dickie and Alicia had become close friends when she was Chief Curator for the American Decorative Arts Department prior to being tapped for the post of Director. She told him to come down at eleven and they could have a coffee.

On the dot of eleven, Dickie was ushered into the Director's Office by her executive secretary. The spacious room's arched windows overlooked Fifth Avenue. An elegant, tall lady rose to meet him. Her dark blonde hair was perfectly coiffed in a flip, and she was chicly dressed in a red Adolfo suit. "Well, Dickie, welcome home," said Alicia. "How was Umbria?"

"It was wonderful beyond my wildest expectations," he replied. "Not only did I have a great rest and change of scene, but—get this—I also discovered a pair of Daniel Fueter candlesticks in a little church near Arabella's villa. Somehow, they're connected with a lady called Adelaide van Wyck. Any idea who she might be?"

"Actually, I do," Alicia replied. "You must remember

her—Mrs. Livingston van Wyck. She's the one who lent the fabulous New York japanned chest and matching dressing table to our 1963 show of colonial furniture in New York collections. She married into a venerable New York Dutch family, and her own family, the Delancys, go way back in the city's history. She's the daughter of the famously wealthy James Schuyler Delancy, who left New York in a fit of pique and moved to Florence around 1910."

"That name's familiar," said Dickie. "Jog my memory?"

"Sure. We know of him here at the Museum because he lent an incredible collection of colonial New York gold hollowware for our 1909 Stuyvesant-Clinton Exhibition."

"Oh yes," Dickie mumbled to himself, "the first Americana show at the Museum."

"That's right."

"Oh, my God," Dickie then exclaimed, "I remember hearing about that legendary gold when I took 'Pots and Pans' at Yale. We were told that it disappeared after the 1909 show here, and that Mr. Garvan had tried in vain to find it."

"Well," continued Alicia, "James Delancy must have taken the gold with him when he moved to Florence, because it apparently was inherited by his son, Philip Schuyler Delancy, who was the brother of Adelaide Delancy van Wyck. I remember coming across a letter about it in the American Department's Promised Gifts and Bequests files, dating—I think—in the late 1930s. His lawyers, Flanigan and Caldwell, wrote to inform us that Philip Delancy planned to leave the entire gold collection to us if he should die without direct heirs. Whatever happened to the gold remains a mystery."

"Really? Nothing?"

"We only know that Delancy died during the Second World War, long before my time here, and we certainly did not receive a bequest of any gold."

"Oh, that's just fascinating. Is Mrs. van Wyck still living?" asked Dickie.

"She is indeed," replied Alicia. "I saw her at the Park Avenue Armory last April during the Preview Party for the Spring Antique Show. She's a very spry and sharp older lady, aged, I would say, in her mid-seventies."

"How do you think I could get an appointment with her?" Dickie asked.

"Well," Alicia responded, "I know her moderately well, as a friend of my parents-in-law, but am not shy about calling to tell her that you recently saw her Fueter candlesticks in the Umbrian church and wanted to come for a visit to learn more about them."

"Gosh, that would be terrific!" said Dickie.

"I'll try to ring her this afternoon," continued Alicia, "but it being mid-summer, she may be away at the van Wyck family camp on Lake Champlain. I think I can maybe find that number in the Social Directory. At any rate, I'll keep you posted."

That afternoon, Alicia rang Dickie in his office, and conveyed to him that she was, indeed, able to reach Mrs. van Wyck at the camp. "That's great news," Dickie said.

"Yes, she was intrigued with the thought of an update on her Fueter candlesticks, as she'd never been to Umbria to see their ultimate location. Here's the bad news—she's not planning to return to the City until the end of the month. She has some important doctor's appointments then."

"Hopefully nothing too serious. That is bad news on top of bad news," Dickie teased.

"I don't think so. Anyway, she said that, when her schedule was more firm, she would ring back and give us several potential times for a meeting."

"That works," said Dickie, though he was admittedly disappointed at having to wait on a tentative meeting.

"And this is interesting," Alicia added. "She knows who you are—she became friends with your mother when they both served on the Board of the Garden Club of America."

"Perfect," Dickie said. "Maybe that means we have an actual chance of hearing back from her."

"Don't be silly," Alicia scolded him with a smile. "Mrs. van Wyck is always true to her word. I'm sure we'll hear from her."

So, in the meanwhile, Dickie decided to make good use of the intervening ten days and do some research on the Delancys and the legendary gold hollowware. He found that the Delancys, of Huguenot descent, arrived in New York in the late seventeenth century. They established a mercantile house specializing in the Triangular Trade between New York, the rich plantation isles of the Caribbean, and the mother country, England. The wealth and prominence of the family in the 1700s was attested by the survival, at the New York Historical Society and other local museums, of portraits by John Wollaston, John Singleton Copley, and Gilbert Stuart. Similarly, their patronage of New York silversmiths, such as Peter van Dyke, Myer Myers, and Daniel Christian Fueter, was reflected in the City Art Museum's own collection by several examples with a Delancy provenance, each engraved with the Delancy arms.

Perhaps the most notable of the colonial Delancys was James Delancy II. Born in 1720, he had risen to lead the family firm by 1760, when he was appointed by the Crown as Lieutenant Governor of the Colony of New York. Shortly after, because of the family's commercial ties with the Caribbean islands, he was appointed Lieutenant Governor of the Bahamas. While in office there, the wreck of a Spanish galleon was discovered off the shore of Great Exuma. The wreck by law belonged to the Crown, but as the Crown's representative, the Royal Governor, Lord Dabney, received a share, as did Lieutenant Governor James Delancy. The wreck included a huge trove of gold bullion.

From a footnote in the 1909 Stuyvesant-Clinton Exhibition catalogue entry on the Delancy gold, Dickie found reference to a contemporary newspaper account of the treasure trove. He was able to locate the original 1764 newspaper in the amazing manuscript collection of the New York Historical Society. Governor James Delancy, the paper noted, sent his share of the gold to New York to the silversmith Daniel Christian Fueter. Fueter had previously been commissioned by Delancy to make various pieces of silver hollowware, including an unusual set of candlesticks rendered in a design that resembled upturned trumpets. Fueter, the article continued, turned the gold into an impressive array of tableware. Included were eight candlesticks, twelve dinner plates, four sauce boats with ladles, one tureen with ladle, twenty-four tablespoons, a cake basket, a large salver, and two smaller waiters. The article concluded with the notation that all the pieces were engraved with the Delancy arms, a blue shield with three gold crescents.

Dickie's mind spun with amazement. The newspaper's listing of forms was exactly the same as the catalogue listing for the 1909 exhibit. How extraordinary, he thought, that in 1909 the collection had survived intact. He wondered if in later decades that still had held true, and if so, maybe it was still all together somewhere. Wouldn't it be a great coup if he could find it and bring it into the City Art Museum's collection, he mused.

August 1980

In early August, Mrs. van Wyck rang Alicia and suggested that Dickie come by in the afternoon for tea three days hence, if that met with Dickie's convenience. She would assume that it was a set date unless she heard to the contrary. Nothing, Dickie thought, could possibly conflict with the appointment.

When the day arrived, Dickie found himself at the corner of 71st Street and Park Avenue. Mrs. van Wyck's address was 71 East 71st Street. Dickie knew from his mother, who was familiar with such things through her Garden Club circle of friends, that this was the discreet side address to New York's most exclusive apartment house, 740 Park Avenue.

Dickie stepped into the marble-floored lobby and was greeted by a doorman smartly attired in a gray uniform that bore the address embroidered in gold on the top edge of the coat pocket. The doorman phoned upstairs to announce Dickie's arrival and then escorted him to the elevator, which was operated by a similarly attired attendant. "Mrs. van Wyck," the doorman told the elevator man. Clearly no further identification was required.

The elevator sped up to the tenth floor, where its doors opened onto the first-floor foyer of Mrs. van Wyck's duplex apartment. The foyer was more like a gallery, extending laterally across the width of the apartment. At one end was a gracious curving staircase leading up to the second floor. The gray-paneled walls were hung with a series of portraits. Dickie recognized a pair of Wollastons, a gentleman and a lady in matching severe black frames, and four Copleys—a boy, a little girl, and a man and woman, probably their parents, as all four bore identical Rococo gilt frames. In addition, there was a pair of Federal-style gilt looking glasses hanging over a pair of Empire-style card tables supported by gilt winged caryatids, obviously Lannuier.

Oh, thought Dickie to himself, *this is going to be very interesting.*

Dickie was greeted by a small gray-haired man attired in a black jacket, gray trousers, white shirt, and black bow tie, all of which indicated that he was the butler. When he spoke, the lilt of his voice further indicated that he was originally from Ireland. "Please come this way," he said. "Mrs. van Wyck will receive you in the drawing room."

Dickie was led down the gallery to a wide, open doorway that gave access to a long room with windows overlooking Park Avenue. The walls were covered in a pale yellow damask, and the modern, comfortable furniture was similarly upholstered. As he entered, he was greeted by a statuesque lady whose graying blonde hair was pulled back in a modified page boy. Her eyes were a piercing hazel. She was attired in a crisp, dark blue linen dress. On either side of the Adam-style fireplace, Dickie espied the japanned high chest and dressing table, the only antique furniture in the room. On the walls, he noticed a pair of Gilbert Stuart portraits and also a pair of portraits that probably were Thomas Sully.

"Good afternoon," his hostess said. "Please come in and have a seat here by the tea table."

"Good afternoon," replied Dickie, going to the tea table and sitting down. "And thank you for agreeing to meet with me."

"Of course. And, by the way, do you mind if I call you by your first name?"

"Yes," he replied, "that would be perfect." Dickie was used to members of his parents' generation being somewhat formal on first acquaintance, so Mrs. van Wyck's request both surprised him and at the same time made him feel very much at ease.

"It might surprise you," Mrs. van Wyck said, "that I do not have my drawing room furnished with Chippendale or Louis Seize, but actually, while I love antiques, I also like to be comfortable, so it's modern sofas and armchairs with fat cushions for me."

Dickie was immediately impressed with her direct manner. As they sat down and she poured tea from a clearly 1920s silver tea set—*probably a wedding present?* he thought—she said to him, "I hear from Alicia that you have recently been in Umbria and seen the family candlesticks I sent there."

"Yes," replied Dickie. "And that led me to you. I was most curious to learn the whole story and how your niece ended up in Italy in the midst of the war."

"Well," Mrs. van Wyck said, "we really need to go back a couple of generations to my father, James Schuyler Delancy. As you may know, in the mid-nineteenth century, the Delancys became involved in the railroad business. My father was the President of the New York Poughkeepsie and Albany Railroad. One day, while en route from New York to Poughkeepsie, my father, who was in his private car, was informed by a conductor that a man in one of the coach cars was repeatedly cursing at a lady passenger. My father went to see what was going on and got into an altercation with the man. He told the man his behavior was uncouth and that it needed to stop immediately. The man then asked my father, 'Who in the hell do you think you are?' Seeking to correct the man's impertinence, my father tweaked his nose. The end result was that the rude man sued my father for assault, and in the subsequent trial, my father was found guilty and fined fifty dollars."

"That's justice for you," Dickie contributed.

Mrs. van Wyck nodded. "As you may have gathered, he was a proud man with a keen belief both in propriety and in the importance of his social position. So, when the decision came down, he was deeply offended. 'Well,' he is said to have proclaimed, 'if this is what my country has come to, I find it no longer a civilized place, and I shall leave it forever.' I was just a little girl of five and my brother, Philip, only two years older. My father moved us lock stock and barrel from New York to a villa in Fiesole, outside Florence. That was in 1910."

"The Villa," she continued, "was first built in the late sixteenth century by a Florentine Prince, and it remained in his family until the mid-nineteenth century when it was sold to an expatriate Englishman, Sir Robert Dalrymple. By that time, the property had fallen into disrepair, and Dalrymple, a man of no small means, poured a fortune into restoring the house and the extensive parterre garden that was cantilevered out over the sloping hill, below the house. The view from the garden overlooked the valley below, with the dome of the Duomo prominent on the horizon. The walls of the three-story villa, plastered in yellow stucco, were accented with gray *pietra serena* around the doorways and fenestration. *Pietra serena* pilasters delineated the corners of the garden façade. Wanting to add a touch of grandeur, Dalrymple erected a tower over the center of the house, echoing those on other Fiesole-area villas with a Medici provenance." Mrs. van Wyck paused, her eyes dreamy, as if she was imagining the sight.

"It sounds pretty grand," Dickie said.

"Indeed. In the mid-1870s, the house gained added distinction when Queen Victoria stayed there during a visit to Florence. All of this made the property very attractive to my father. After extended negotiations with the Dalrymple descendants, he secured its purchase. So, when we were little, we lived there, with my parents and a vast staff of servants. There were no other American families, but there were a number of English ones living in neighboring villas. Several titled Florentine families also had villas nearby. They became friends of my parents, and their children our playmates. For the first five or six years, we were educated at home by a strict English schoolmaster. When Philip reached the age of thirteen, he was sent back to America to enter the first form at St. Paul's School in New Hampshire. His vacations were spent in New York with my paternal aunt, Sarah Schuyler Delancy, and her husband, Hamilton Bostwick. In the summers, Phillip returned to us in Fiesole."

"You must have missed him during the school year," Dickie said.

"I did. Several years later, I was entered into the Ethel Walker School in Connecticut, and my life followed a similar pattern. After Philip graduated from Harvard, he decided to return permanently to Fiesole. I, on the other hand, during the year I made my debut in New York, fell in love with and married Livingston van Wyck. So, I became a permanent New Yorker. And here I still am."

"In the mid-nineteen twenties," she continued, "just after Phillip returned to live in Fiesole, he was introduced to a young girl visiting from England. She was a guest of the Lord and Lady Wessington, expatriates who lived in the villa next to ours. The girl, Alexandra, had an interesting history. She was the daughter of Ernest Gruene, an Ashkenazi Jew who, as a young man, emigrated from Germany to London and entered the banking business. He was enormously successful, and amassed a huge fortune. Gruene became both a lender to, and a friend of the Prince of Wales as well as his wife, Alexandra. In 1903, Gruene, who had anglicized his name to Greene and converted to Christianity, married the Honorable Margaret Dinsmore, daughter of the Lord Angus Dinsmore. Two years later, the then-King made his friend the first Baron Greene of Wenham. It was also in 1905 that Lady Margaret gave birth to their daughter and only child. She was named Alexandra, in honor of the Queen.

"Alexandra Greene was tall and slim, with jet-black hair and deep brown, nearly black eyes. My brother, in contrast, was very blond with pale blue eyes. They made a striking couple. It wasn't long before the two fell deeply in love. Word of their relationship and the desire to marry soon became known both to my parents in Fiesole and to the Greenes in London. Neither couple was happy with the prospect. The

Greenes were not at all keen on the idea of an American commoner as a son-in-law, despite the fact that he was quite wealthy. The Delancys were equally opposed to their only son and heir marrying an English girl who was half Jewish. My brother reminded our parents that in the seventeen hundreds, our ancestor Oliver Delancy had married Phila Franks, the daughter of Sephardic Jews living in New York. While this was not a reminder my parents relished, they realized that it weakened the premise of their objections. As a compromise, both sets of parents agreed to the marriage, but only if Philip and Alexandra would wait for five years. In 1930, the couple finally married in a small private ceremony at Saint Mark's, the English church in Florence. Three years later, my niece, also named Alexandra, was born. She was their only child."

Dickie thought this a very interesting tale, and it began to explain how the girl, Alexandra, ended up in Camerata, but what he really wanted to learn was the story of the fabled gold—once it left New York (if in fact it did) and then if so, what happened to it in Florence. But he was too polite to interrupt his hostess's narrative, so he sat back, all ears.

Just as this thought crossed his mind, he heard Mrs. van Wyck say, "You probably are eager to have me tell you about the gold. I'll get to that in a moment, but I think it important that you understand what happened in the thirties and then during the war. My brother and his wife became leading members of a circle of expats and Florentine aristocracy. Included also were, of course, well-connected Italians who were at the same time fascists. That fact did not bother Philip. He thought their connections would protect his family, although they were in fact alien nationals. Their closest friends and confidants were the Principe and Principessa Chiravalle, Filippo and Maria Pia. They were in fact godparents to Alexandra.

"At the outbreak of the World War in the fall of 1939, the Delancys were living in the Fiesole villa. Philip, having spent most of his life in Fiesole, saw no need to leave, as America was not involved and his English wife had earlier taken American citizenship. When the United States entered the war in December of 1941, the Delancys suddenly felt trapped but still thought the connections with their fascist friends would protect them. What happened next," Mrs. van Wyck related, "I only learned later from friends in the State Department.

"After the Italian surrender to the Allies in September of 1943, all changed, and Florence was completely dominated by the occupying German forces. Nazi politics and policies ruled, including anti-Semitism. The Germans turned the historic via Farini Synagogue into a warehouse and a stable. They began to deport prominent Jews, starting with the chief rabbi, and at the same time began appropriating art from private collections. In late February of 1944, Philip apparently discussed the situation with his close friend Maria Pia Chiravalle, and she agreed that the Germans represented great danger. She told him of her plan to evacuate the Chiravalle paintings down to Umbria. Philip apparently asked her if she might also be able to evacuate her goddaughter, Alexandra. We don't know whether or not he made arrangements about the Delancy gold. It seems that the princess agreed to this plan, and Alexandra was sent to the Palazzo Chiravalle, to be hidden there temporarily.

"The Delancys were very well known in Florentine society, so as aliens they soon came to the attention of the German officials. It was only a few days after hiding their daughter that they both were arrested by the Gestapo. I learned later," Mrs. van Wyck continued, "that my brother was accused of being an American spy. My sister-in-law was arrested for being half Jewish. Their villa and all its contents were confiscated by the Nazis. Both Philip and Alexandra were deported to Auschwitz, where they later perished."

"Goodness," interjected Dickie, "their story is both fascinating and at the same time tragic. The memory must be difficult for you."

"That is true," Mrs. van Wyck replied as she continued. "We were told after the war by friends in the State Department that Princess Chiravalle knew she had to act immediately to implement her plan, not only for the paintings but also for my niece. Time was of the essence as the Germans had begun to take a census of all Florentine households. The paintings were relatively simple, my niece a greater problem. Fortunately, in early March, her close Roman friend, Dottore Piero Galeassi-Lisi, was visiting in Florence. As personal physician to the Pope, the occupying German authorities treated him with respect and allowed him relatively unsupervised travel. The doctor agreed to escort young Alexandra from Florence to Orvieto and thence to his villa near Fiore, where the princess's staff would take over."

"So," concluded Mrs. van Wyck, "that is how my niece ended up in Umbria in the midst of the war. I understand from Alicia Milhaus that you learned the rest of the story while you were there last month. After the war we learned—also from friends in the State Department—about Alexandra's last days, but they knew nothing about the gold. What happened to the gold, I do not know. I remember that my father had six specially designed, leather-covered carrying cases built at the time we moved from America, and these accompanied us along with our normal luggage when we sailed from New York to Le Havre and then traveled on by train to Florence. My father displayed the gold in a small, locked, vaulted, treasury-like room at the villa. Its presence was semi-secret and only the most privileged guests were given the opportunity to see it. When I was about ten, I remember my father being insulted when the silver collector Francis Garvan had the gall to send his secretary to make a huge cash offer of purchase. Of course, it was not for sale. The carrying cases were still around in our luggage storeroom when I was growing up, so I would assume my brother could have used them when, we think, he removed the gold from the villa prior to his arrest. But then, maybe not."

"So you have no idea where the gold might be now?" said Dickie, hopefully.

Mrs. van Wyck shook her head and took a sip of tea. "Maybe it became part of the Nazi loot, and for all I know was maybe melted down. At any rate, it seems to have completely disappeared. After the war, through an intermediary, we made an overture to the Princess Chiravalle to find out what she knew about the gold, but were informed that she was critically ill with cancer and not available to speak with us. No one else at the Palazzo Chiravalle had any knowledge of what happened to the gold during the war. So, we have always assumed it was lost forever."

Well, thought Dickie, *I guess my quest for a once-in-a-lifetime curatorial coup in finding and acquiring the fabled Delancy gold has just hit a dead end.*

3

MANHATTAN

October 1980

S oon after Dickie's mid-July return from Umbria, he politely wrote a letter of thanks to his hosts, the di Florianos. Then, still a bit intrigued with the sexy Marchesa, he also wrote a letter to Lucrezia Atti, thanking her for the splendid dinner at Crispiano, and for sharing with him the saga of her grandmother's rescue of the family paintings. "You mentioned to me," he wrote, "that your grandmother kept meticulous records. I wonder if there might be any reference to her taking in the American girl. I learned here in New York, from the girl's aunt, that your grandparents were her godparents. Apparently, the girl's father had an incredible collection of colonial American gold hollowware. It seems to have disappeared during the war. I wonder if, while rescuing the girl, somehow the gold was also rescued?"

Six weeks later, Dickie received a short response from Lucrezia. After saying how much she enjoyed meeting him, she apologized for the delay in response. She explained she had intended to get up to Florence, but a trip to London to visit her two children who were in boarding school there had intervened. She hoped, she wrote, that she would be able to go up soon.

Dickie, while happy to have the response that Lucrezia enjoyed meeting him, was also disappointed that he would have to wait for anything further about the gold, if in fact it still did exist and if there were any clues buried in the princess's papers. He wrote back a hasty note thanking her, and expressing the hope of hearing from her soon. The fall season was upon the Museum with its usual flurry of post-summer exhibits and events, as well as the demanding but necessary monthly meetings with his trustee committee. So, he mentally put the gold idea in remote mental storage.

Several weeks later, he received another letter from Umbria. "I think I have some promising news," Lucrezia wrote. "I went up to Florence last week. The Palazzo, as you may know, was inherited by my uncle Prince Carlo Chiravalle, after my grandfather's death in 1950. His wife, Princess Amelia, is a very difficult person and not fond of me, so I do not have completely free access to things. But I am friendly with the current archivist, who is called Luigi Giovanelli—he is the son of the archivist in my grandmother's time. I did have a good meeting with him. I explained that an American curator was interested in the story of my grandmother's wartime rescue of the family pictures, and the concurrent rescue of an American girl. I asked him if he knew of any pertinent documents in my grandmother's papers. 'Well,' he responded, 'interesting you should ask. As you know the painting collection has been under an extensive program of conservation for the last almost ten years. The project is expected to be completed next year, and in 1982 a completely new and fully researched catalogue will be ready for publication. There also will be a gala opening of the collection's reinstallation in the picture gallery in March 1982. That year also marks the thirty-fifth anniversary of Princess Maria Pia's 1947 death from cancer. An important essay in the catalogue will consider her life and her role in saving the collection. I know the author is now doing research in your grandmother's papers. She is away from Florence at the moment, but when she returns in two weeks' time, I will speak to her. In the meanwhile, I can, on my own, do some sleuthing.' So," the letter concluded, "we will await word from Giovanelli."

Well, thought Dickie to himself, *maybe there is a glimmer of hope that some light might be shed on what actually happened in the early spring of 1944.*

November 1980

Dickie was very surprised and excited when, upon return to the apartment after work, he found a letter from Umbria in his mailbox. He restrained himself from ripping it open in the elevator, but as soon as the elevators doors closed on his front hall, he raced to the living room, sat down, and opened the letter.

Dated November 3, 1980, and written on Crispiano stationary embossed with an engraved crest, the letter began with "Dearest Dickie," and that warm salutation made him smile to himself as he felt a small surge of happiness. The letter continued, "I had a call from my friend the archivist, who told me he thought he had come across something. He didn't want to commit anything to writing, as he was working sort of *sub rosa* without my aunt's knowledge or approval. To avoid attracting her attention, he suggested that I make a casual visit to the Palazzo and simply drop in on his office, ostensibly to have a friendly chat. So, day before yesterday, I drove up under the guise of having lunch with my other aunt, Countess Anna Maria di Baldini. I parked in the Palazzo courtyard and walked to the nearby restaurant. After lunch, I made my casual stop at the Palazzo to visit the archivist before retrieving my car. When I got to his tiny office, located under the eaves on the top floor of the Palazzo, he beckoned me in and shut the door. After we sat down, he told me he had been reviewing my grandmother's daily diary for late February and early March of 1944, the time when the transfer of the paintings was being organized. He found, he related, several cryptic entries, written in the code she used to assure privacy on sensitive matters. 'My father,' he continued, 'told me that the code was very simple. It substituted numbers for letters, starting backwards in the alphabet with Z. So, I was able to translate, and this is what I found: For March 3, 1944: ASD/PG–L/Umbria, and for March 5: Paintings 6 cases Mariano Sant' Ilario.' Clearly, the first reference is to Alexandra Delancy, whose middle name we just discovered was Schuyler, and the Holy Father's doctor, Piero Galeazzi-Lisi. The second entry and reference to paintings is also clear. We know they were hidden at Castello Mariano and we know she left the art in care of Sant' Ilario, but what '6 cases' means is a mystery. So, although we did find something about the girl, I am afraid what we found was no help in solving the mystery of what happened to the gold. I wish I could have better news, but then, there it is." The letter concluded, "With all warmest wishes, and love, Lucrezia."

"Bingo!" Dickie shouted. His mind began to race. *Six cases' jibes exactly with what Mrs. van Wyck remembered being custom-made for movement of the Delancy gold. So that entry suggests that the gold, packed in its traveling cases, was probably transferred from the Delancy villa to the Palazzo Chiravalle, and then sent down to the Castello Mariano at the same time as the Chiravalle painting collection.* Dickie could hardly contain his excitement. His immediate thought was to phone Lucrezia to convey to her how important the reference to "six cases" was, but then remembering the time difference between New York and Italy decided that discretion was the better part of valor, so he would wait until the next morning and phone before going to work.

As soon as he woke up, he rummaged through his desk for the little red, Morocco leather-covered book in which he kept European phone numbers. While in Umbria, he had added not only the di Florianos, but on a whim, also got the number at Crispiano. He rehearsed what he would say in Italian if someone other than Lucrezia answered, and then direct dialed. After a pause, the connection was made and the phone on the other end began to ring. And it rang and rang. Dickie was about to hang up when someone finally responded.

"*Pronto.*"

"Lucrezia?" Dickie inquired.

"*No, sono Stefanella.*"

"*Ce la Marchesa?*" responded Dickie.

"*Mi scusi, ma non ce, e fuori,*" was the answer.

"*Per favore, dica a la Marchesa che Dickie da America a telefonato.*"

From the other end he heard "*Va bene*" and a click as the connection was cut off. So, he learned that Lucrezia was not home. He hoped that the message that he had called was understood.

Well, thought Dickie, *that was not very productive.* Now he would have to wait, because he didn't want to call from work and Lucrezia didn't have his office number. *But wait,* he thought, reconsidering. *This is important museum work, so it's totally legit to call from the office.*

Later in the morning, he phoned Crispiano again, and that time Lucrezia answered. He explained to her his theory of the six cases. She responded she was excited for him that there might be a lead. She promised to contact the people at both the Palazzo and also at Mariano who were involved when the paintings at Mariano were repatriated. As the gold was maybe hidden at the same time, perhaps someone would have information that shed light on what may have happened to the six cases.

December 1980

Weeks had gone by with no news from Umbria, but while Dickie was frustrated, he was loath to bug Lucrezia. She was, after all, doing him a favor.

At last, in the week before Christmas, he found a letter from Lucrezia in the apartment post box. "I have spoken with some of the elderly staff at Mariano and also the Palazzo and asked them about the process when the paintings were repatriated to Florence," Lucrezia wrote. "There was a fairly clear recollection of the sealed-off space in the depths of the castle, and the careful process of taking inventory as the individual paintings were brought out. According to what I was able to find, no one saw anything other than the paintings in the secret space. My query about cases that maybe looked like luggage did not ring a bell with anyone. So, I'm afraid I have failed you and we are at a dead end."

Well, thought Dickie, *I guess that is that, and I should get on with life and my work at the Museum.*

4

MANHATTAN

January 1981

A few weeks after New Year's, Dickie found, on his return home from work, a letter from Umbria waiting in his mailbox. As he had not expected to hear anything further, he was mildly surprised. After he fixed himself a Stoli on the rocks, he settled down in the living room and opened the letter.

"Dearest Dickie," it began. Again, he experienced a surge of warmth. Then he read on. "You may remember me telling you, Mariano belongs to my Uncle Carlo. At *Natale*, he always has a family gathering there, with a mass in the chapel dedicated to our patron saint, Sant' Ilario. Afterwards, there is a family luncheon. During the Mass, I remembered my grandmother's daybook reference to the Sant' Ilario, which we all thought pertained to his protecting the paintings. It got me to wondering if instead it meant the chapel, and that we might be looking in the wrong place for the hidden gold.

Later, at lunch, when I explained your quest to my uncle and mentioned the idea of the gold maybe being hidden in the chapel, my Aunt Amelia immediately interrupted. She firmly stated that under no circumstances could the sanctity of the family chapel be violated for some American wild goose chase. My uncle, who is dominated by Amelia, said he agreed. So, I thought that was the end of it. After all, it was only an idea."

"However," the letter continued, "I was irritated by my aunt's proprietary attitude, so I decided that after the holidays I would make some discreet inquiries to the Palazzo archives. I was sure that the architectural records for the chapel's construction would be filed there, and they might reveal if there were any hidden or secret spaces. Much to my dismay, I learned that my aunt had already visited the archives and commanded that all papers pertaining to the construction of the chapel be given to her. I don't know what she is up to, but I do know she is a greedy person, and she may think that if it exists she can get her hands on the gold for herself. But I do have friends among the staff at Mariano, and I have asked them to alert me if my aunt has instructed Mariano staff to undertake any exploratory activity within the chapel. I'll keep you posted. Love, Lucrezia"

Well, thought Dickie, *the plot thickens.*

Florence, February 1981

Amelia, Principessa Chiravalle, a stocky short woman with curly close-cropped gray hair, was widely known throughout aristocratic Italian circles—not only in Florence but also Rome as well as Umbria—as a difficult person. Born into a venerable but impoverished Florentine noble family, she exulted in her marital status and wore her "princess" title on her sleeve. She was quick to respond to anything she viewed as a slight to either herself or to her husband's family. So, when she heard from her niece, Lucrezia (whom she felt never showed the proper respect), that there was the possibility of valuable gold hidden in her husband's property, she determined that something of such value—if it could be found—would not be lost to some unknown Americans. So, she began a secret campaign to search for the potential treasure.

Upon her return to Florence after the Christmas holiday at Mariano, she sent for the family archivist, Luigi Giovanelli, and instructed him to locate and bring to her all papers pertaining to the construction of the family's Sant' Ilario Chapel in the *borgo* at Mariano. To her annoyance, she was told by the archivist that this might take some time, as everyone was busy with the project on the painting collection. She responded that her project should become his number one priority. "When you find the chapel plans," she told him, " I want them brought immediately to me. And I will need someone to read them for me."

The following week, the archivist asked for an appointment. Eager to learn what news he brought, Amelia dropped everything in her schedule for that day and asked that he be sent to her apartments.

"I am afraid," the archivist told her, "that I have not yet been able to locate the original plans for the Church of Sant' Ilario at Mariano. I did, however, run across correspondence between the Principessa Maria Pia and her Mariano steward, Michele Ricci, dating from the latter part of the war. She asked him to find a place to hide a valuable shipment that would be arriving from Florence. A later letter from Ricci informed her that he had been able to successfully fulfill her request, and mentioned that there were some minor expenses for work in the chapel on masonry, and that an estimate of the expenses would follow. However," he continued, "we have not yet been able to find that document, so we do not know what work was done or its location."

Amelia was excited to hear this information, but she did not want the archivist to know that she was hoping to find hidden gold. What she did not know, however, was that because of the earlier requests from Lucrezia Atti, the archives staff were already aware of the fact that some gold may have been hidden at Mariano. Like Lucrezia, with this new information they made the connection between the Principessa Maria Pia's cryptic notation "6 cases Mariano Sant' Ilario" and the church dedicated to him.

The Church of Sant' Ilario di Chiravalle was erected in the second half of the sixteenth century to comply with the Pope's instruction to build a church in honor of the family's newly canonized ancestor. He had been a much beloved medieval bishop in Lucca. However, in accordance with the Prince Chiravalle's desire not to expend huge amounts of money on something he did not really want or need, the church was neither large, nor elegant, nor in a recognizable style. Built of local fieldstone, it was a simple rectangle relieved by a small apse at the far end. Two small sub-chapels, for family devotion, flanked the altar located within the apse. The interior was severely plain, with no expensive marble ornament, or frescos. The terracotta tile roof was supported by a massive beam and truss system made of chestnut. The floor was paved with large, simple squares of gray stone. In the area beneath the altar, there was a small crypt where the remains of the newly canonized family ancestor were transferred after completion of the church.

Encouraged by the newfound correspondence, which suggested that the gold had in fact been somehow hidden in the family chapel, Amelia frantically began to scheme—how might she be able to locate it without anyone else knowing? She was not sure if there were any staff at the Florence Palazzo in whom she could confide and enlist their aid. There might, she thought, be one person at Mariano, an attractive young man who was assistant to the steward. She had accidently learned that he was having an affair with another young man in the *borgo. So*, she thought, *that might provide the needed leverage.* She had also once noticed her young chauffeur eying the steward's assistant, and she kept that in mind as another avenue of leverage. When she would need to make her trip down to Mariano to find the gold, she wanted it to be secret.

What remained was a valid reason for the trip, an excuse for why she would be going. That would require careful planning.

In the meantime, for the archivist, who for years had been treated with arrogance and rudeness by Principessa Amelia, there was little love lost and no feeling of loyalty to his mistress. Over the years, he had, however, a wonderful, warm working relationship with her sister-in-law, Maria Christina Chiravalle Bianchini, and Maria Christina's daughter, Lucrezia Bianchini Atti. He felt obligated, therefore, to contact Lucrezia and bring her up to date on the recently discovered letters. Not willing to depend on the *Poste Italiano*, which was notably unreliable as well as incredibly slow, he steeled himself to take the risk, and telephoned Crispiano.

Manhattan, Late February 1981

Dickie was just finishing his morning meal—black coffee and a hard roll slathered with butter and honey—when the apartment phone rang. He was, to his surprise, greeted by the musical voice of Lucrezia Atti.

"Oh, *pronto*, Dickie," she breathlessly began, "I have very interesting and exciting news. I would have rung you last night, but I got confused about the time difference, so waited until today. Two days ago, I received a call from Giovanelli, the Palazzo's archivist, who told me that he had discovered letters written in 1944 between my grandmother and her Mariano steward. They contained clear reference to what must be the gold, and that it was to be hidden in the Church of Sant' Ilario at Mariano. He also warned me that my Aunt Amelia is hot on the trail of the potential treasure. As you may know, Dickie, I do not have any official connection with Mariano. But as it is the family's ancestral seat, I can occasionally and casually have access to the property. I have always maintained good relations with the staff there. I right away rang the steward, Bruno Caparoli, who is in fact the brother-in-law of my steward here at Crispiano, Sandro Trotti, and asked if he might have time to meet with me on a sensitive family matter."

"Wow, Lucrezia," Dickie interjected, "this sounds very exciting, I can't wait to hear more."

Lucrezia continued. "I drove over yesterday and met him in his office for a coffee. I told him the whole story, or as much of it as I know. I started with my grandmother's transferal of the family paintings down to Mariano in early 1944, something he already was aware of. I didn't go into the saga of the lost girl, although as a local, he has probably heard that tale. But I did then explain that close friends of my grandmother had entrusted a large suite of gold tableware to her safekeeping from the occupying German forces in Florence. There is evidence that the gold was sent down to Mariano at the same time as the paintings, and that recently uncovered letters in my grandmother's papers at the Palazzo strongly suggest that the gold was hidden somewhere in the family chapel, Sant' Ilario. I also let Bruno know he should be aware, as I had it on good authority, that my aunt, wife of his boss, was very interested in retrieving the gold for herself. The gold, if it should be found, rightfully belongs to an important museum in New York."

"Did he agree?" asked Dickie.

"Yes, without hesitation. As with practically everyone else who has had to work with her," Lucrezia continued, "Bruno Caparoli has experienced the arrogance and abuse directed at him by the sharp tongue of my aunt. So, he did not see a problem with my suggestion that we keep our meeting and this information to ourselves. We laid plans to visit the chapel and look around to see if there were any visible clues."

"I'm relieved to hear you have him on your side, Lucrezia!"

"Me too," Lucrezia replied. "And we didn't waste any time either. We left his office, came out through the curtain wall of the castle, and walked down the street that encircles the wall, until we came to the entrance of the chapel. Bruno unlocked the heavy wooden door. The interior is very plain, so it didn't offer many possibilities for hiding places. As we walked around, it seemed to us that somewhere near the altar—maybe one of the little side chapels or even the crypt—might be possibilities. We tentatively tapped on the walls to see if anything sounded hollow, but found nothing. We realized we would need assistance, maybe from a mason or someone with professional expertise, like an architect or archaeologist. So that would have to wait for another day. After I got home, I remembered the young son of a good friend, an American married to a Neapolitan Count, who lives across the Tiber from us. Their son, Francesco Orsini, who was trained as an architect in America, has done a lot of work in the area restoring old farmhouses and villas as vacation homes for English and American clients. So, I think he might be able to help us.

I just need to set up a meeting and explain discreetly what I have in mind. I hope, with his being half American, that the connection to your museum will help make him receptive to the project. So, dear Dickie, that is all I know at the moment," Lucrezia concluded.

"Oh, my God, that is so exciting!" responded Dickie. "Do you think I should come over and help with the search?"

"As much as I would like that," she replied, "I am afraid your presence would attract attention and that soon would get to my aunt. The very walls have ears here, and news travels fast. I promise you, as soon as we find something, if we have that good fortune, I will call you, day or night. Then it would be good for you to come. We'll talk again soon; I send you *bacis*. Bye now."

As Dickie hung up, he could not decide which excited him more, the news that discovery might be in sight, or that Lucrezia had sent him kisses. In his excitement, he completely missed the fact that Lucrezia's American friend, was, as his mother had told him, a cousin by marriage. Dickie said to himself, *Oh, of course—the Orsinis. They are the cousins Mother told me about last summer.*

He raced to get dressed and off to the Museum. As soon as he got to his office, he rang Alicia Milhaus to get her up to date on the recent developments. She suggested that he come down to her office. There, over coffee, he summarized the information Lucrezia's phone conversation had supplied just an hour earlier. Alicia agreed that it was indeed interesting and maybe even promising. "But if it is found," she cautioned, "there might be problems in the gold being turned over to the

Museum. In my experience, nothing to do with Italy and its entrenched bureaucracy is simple."

"I'm slowly learning this," Dickie agreed.

"You just need to be prepared for a long road ahead, if we do have good fortune and the gold is finally found. And, more importantly, if we can provide legal evidence to support the Museum's claim."

"How do we go about doing that?" asked Dickie.

"I don't know. I think it might be a good idea if I rang Bobby Satterthwaite, the Museum's counsel at Delano and Pomeroy, and ask his advice on how to proceed, should we get to that point."

Dickie saw the wisdom in Alicia's advice, but even so was eager to do something to move the situation ahead. He realized, however, that any progress in Umbria depended on his new friend Lucrezia Atti, and that he would have to wait it out in New York.

Umbria, a Few Days Later

After Lucrezia's phone conversation with Dickie—morning his time, afternoon hers—she rang Countess Sara Orsini and asked for the studio phone number of her son, Francesco. Sara was only too happy to supply the information—Lucrezia guessed that the countess sensed a potential new client for her son. As it was late in the day, Lucrezia decided to wait until the next day to place the call. First thing the next morning, she rang Francesco Orsini's studio in Perugia. She opened by explaining who she was, as the two had never actually met. Francesco Orsini, however, knew exactly who she was.

"Oh, Marchesa," Orsini interjected, "but I do know who you are, as I have often heard Mummy speak of you."

Lucrezia continued. "I have an unusual request for a project, one difficult to discuss via phone. Would it be possible for you to come to Crispiano to talk further?" Lucrezia asked. She could sense that her somewhat cryptic call had aroused Francesco's curiosity, though Francesco resisted suggesting an immediate meeting. "Would the day after tomorrow work for you, Marchesa?"

"*Va bene*," she replied. "Shall we say ten?"

Lucrezia had recommended that he arrive a few minutes early, allowing time to park in the *borgo* and walk up the street to the curtain wall entrance and thence into a large courtyard outside the exterior castle wall. He must have taken her advice, because he was there right on time—Lucrezia met him by the main door off the courtyard.

Francesco Orsini looked to be in his early thirties. He was of medium height and narrow-shouldered, with close cropped, wiry blond hair. She escorted him up the magnificent gray stone staircase and to the vaulted *salotto*, where they sat down in comfortable overstuffed armchairs. After coffee was served, Lucrezia began her story. She was not sure whether she was making a mistake to trust this young man, but she knew that she needed to be candid if she was going to convince the young architect to assist her in finding out where in the church they might find the hidden gold.

In the course of her narration, she mentioned that her role in all this was to help a friend who was a curator at the City Art Museum in New York. "Oh, really, who's that?" inquired Francesco.

"Dickie Read," Lucrezia replied.

"Goodness, that is so amazing!" Francesco exclaimed. "Mummy just recently told me that Dickie Read, a cousin by marriage, was an important curator at that museum. What a small world! So, by helping you, I would be helping my cousin. I would like to do that if I can."

After Lucrezia finished laying out the story, she outlined the need to examine the church at Mariano for possible evidence of where the gold might be hidden. Francesco responded, "I know a wonderful old master mason who has worked for me on several restorations. But even better, he is often retained by the Belle Arti for work on historic buildings and churches. He is called Enzo Sebastiano," Francesco continued. "We're not working together on a project at the moment, but when I get back to my studio, I can ring him and see if he might be available to meet with us at Mariano sometime in the next few days. How does that sound to you?"

"Wonderful," was her reply. "I look forward to your call and will leave my schedule open until I hear."

After Francesco departed, Lucrezia mused to herself, *Belle Arti, hmm, I had not thought about them. Since the Church of Sant' Ilario is a historic structure, and the gold antique, we might have a problem there. Well, we can cross that bridge when we get to it.*

5

FLORENCE

Early March

Amelia Chiravalle, who was a keen gardener, took both immense interest and huge pride in the world famous Giardino Chiravalle at a family villa in Fiesole. Originally laid out in the early seventeenth century, the elaborate parterre garden was renowned in the twentieth century as probably the best-preserved surviving example from the Italian Renaissance. As it was now early spring, Amelia resumed her weekly trips up from Florence to consult with the gardening staff as the gardens awoke from their winter slumber.

For these trips up to Fiesole, Amelia like to travel in her husband's Mercedes limousine, even though he warned her that, because of the ever-present threat from terrorists like the Red Brigades, it was not safe. The Chiravalles were not immune to the attention of the Red Brigades. In Florence's business circles, Carlo was well known as President and a major owner of the huge insurance firm Assicurazione Toscana. The family's wealth was legendary, so Carlo was a prime target for kidnapping. Aware of the possibility, he eschewed his Mercedes 600 L limousine and his beloved Ferrari Testa Rosa for a humble tiny Fiat. Amelia, however, proud of their luxury vehicles, continued at times to travel in the Mercedes limousine.

The distinctive burgundy-colored limousine, with Amelia aboard, shot out of the Palazzo gate and onto the Lungarno, and thence sped east through the narrow streets of old Florence toward the wide road that climbed the hills at the edge of the city and led up to Fiesole. Much to her alarm, she noticed a pair of black-clad, helmeted riders following them on *motorinos*. They were soon joined by two more. The four *motorinos* began to flank the large car and, as they got closer, attempted to force it into a dead-end side street. The four men brandished pistols, and Amelia shook with terror as the chauffeur followed their gestured instructions and turned into the side street. A black van simultaneously appeared and blocked the end of the side street. More masked and armed men sprang out of the van and raced over to the blocked limousine. "We've got him," one of the men yelled, as he wrenched open the door of the car. Then, espying Amelia cowering in the back seat, yelled, "*Merda*, it's some woman, not the old *principe!*"

"Never mind," the apparent leader said. "She must be worth something. Let's take her! *Viva le Brigate Rosse!*" With that, Amelia was hauled out of the Mercedes and bundled into the waiting van, which then sped away, followed by the four *motorinos*. It all happened in less than ninety seconds.

Amelia was fairly sure her chauffer, while terrified, had not been harmed. She was certain that as soon as he got over the shock and got his head around what had happened and realized that she had been kidnapped by the Red Brigades, he would make his way back to the Palazzo and report what had happened to the steward, who would ring Principe Carlo at his office to relay the dire news. That was her only hope of getting out of this scenario, she thought, as the black van made its way out to the edges of the city and into an industrial zone where there were dozens of anonymous warehouses. As the van pulled up to one, located on a remote interior street, the doors swung open and it pulled in, the doors closing behind it.

Amelia was dragged out of the van and led to a small room within the larger space. It was completely bare save for a table and a wooden chair, a squalid mattress on the floor, and a bucket in the corner. While she was terrified, Amelia did notice that all her captors seemed to be very young men. Handheld radios provided communication with each other, and apparently with their superiors. Ever a pragmatic person, she knew exactly what she had gotten herself into, and her mind began to race. *I know they are in it for the money*, she thought. *How can I safely capitalize on that? And they are young, too—maybe they are somehow vulnerable. How can I quickly get access to something of enough value to barter for my release?*

Umbria, Early March

Francesco Orsini rang Lucrezia Atti several days after their meeting at Crispiano. "I contacted the mason, Sebastiano, and laid out for him what we needed," he said, "and he told me that he would be happy to visit Mariano and assist me and you in examining the chapel there. He and I tentatively settled on the day after tomorrow, in the morning," continued Orsini, "if that would work for you."

"I think that would be fine," responded Lucrezia, "but I need to clear our visit with the steward, as he is ultimately responsible for the property. May I get back to you?"

"*Certo*," was the reply.

Lucrezia rang Bruno Caparoli at Mariano and they set the meeting for ten o'clock two days later. That information was then passed on to Francesco, who agreed to relay the news to the mason.

Mid-morning of the selected day found the party—the architect, the mason, the steward and the Marchesa—at the entrance to the Church of Sant' Ilario in Il Castello di Mariano. Bruno Caparoli unlocked the stout wooden door and they proceeded inside. They agreed that somewhere at the altar end of the church was the best place to start.

Enzo Sebastiano's practiced eye examined the stonework of the walls, both around the altar and inside the two side chapels. He did not detect any anomalies. They decided, therefore, to look further, down in the crypt. With only a little bit of light from the entrance above, the crypt was, of course, a very dark space. Fortunately, Enzo had brought a portable lighting device that had a very powerful beam. It also could be switched to an ultraviolet mode, which in the darkness would show any differences in the mortar. They descended the steep stone steps to the lower level, and walked slowly around the perimeter of the space as Enzo carefully examined the ashlar blocks of the walls. At the end of their circuit they were standing in the far end of the crypt at the head of the Saint's tomb.

"*Niente*," Enzo grunted. "*Mi scusi*, but I do not see mortar that is at variance with the masonry around it, which is what I would expect if someone had opened a wall to create a hiding space behind the surface."

"*O, mio Dio. Niente?*" said Lucrezia, who was standing directly on an axis with the Saint's tomb. "How frustrating!" She stomped her foot, annoyed. The impact created a dull, but clearly hollow sound. The group was struck silent for a moment.

Lucrezia could not contain her excitement. Was this it?

Enzo began to tap with a small mallet that he had brought just for this purpose, and again there was a hollow sound. He turned on the ultraviolet mode of his device and carefully examined the mortar around the four, square paving stones on which they were standing. "*Si si*," he said, "look here, the mortar around these stones does not fluoresce the same as that on the adjacent ones. This means it was not put there at the same time as the other mortar. I think we may have found the hiding place. But we will need equipment to raise the stones. I can bring that down from Perugia. Before I begin,

I will need written permission to move the stones. Does the Belle Arti know what you are planning?"

Bruno and Lucrezia had anticipated the requirement for written permission, which Bruno thought he could provide without the knowledge of Principessa Amelia. He simply would, after the fact, inform the *principe* that there had been a small problem in the flooring around the Saint's tomb, which he had taken the liberty of seeing to. However, the Belle Arti represented a serious problem. The organization had wide sweeping powers over any changes to, or work on historic buildings, not only public but also private. Unfortunately, the church fell under their purview. Lucrezia deeply hoped to avoid the bureaucratic delays—application for permission, inspections, the approval process, final permission, and onsite supervision—that Belle Arti involvement would entail. They decided to follow the usual Italian *modus vivendi* with bureaucracy, which was to ignore the rules until caught, and then pay whatever *condono*, or fine, was involved.

Florence, a Day Later

As Amelia Chiravalle had planned a full day outside in the Fiesole garden, supervising the spring preparations, she had dressed warmly in wool slacks, a wool jumper, and a quilted jacket. Knowing that the ground would be either wet, or worse, muddy, she wore sturdy rubber shoes. In addition, she had removed her six carat rose-cut diamond engagement ring, leaving her hands only adorned with her plain gold wedding band and a gold signet ring inset with carnelian, which was engraved with the Chiravalle crest. As she would be working, she saw no need to take a purse with her.

The fact that she was warmly dressed stood Amelia in good stead, as the corrugated steel warehouse in which she now was incarcerated had no heat. While it had started out as a balmy spring day, as night fell, the temperature dropped dramatically. The bare dank cement floor offered no comfort, so she was obliged to either sit or lie on the fetid mattress, as the chair and table were continuously occupied, in shifts, by a foot soldier of the Red Brigades. She soon swallowed her pride and relieved herself in the bucket that was set in the corner.

While Amelia tried to strike up a conversation with her guards, the young men were singularly uncommunicative. It was not until the next morning, when an apparent superior came into the room, that anyone spoke to her directly. The middle-aged man was dressed in black from head to toe and wore a black face mask. "*Signora*," he began, "who are you? You have no identity papers."

"Of course I don't," Amelia haughtily replied. "I left them at home because I was going to spend a day gardening."

"Watch your tongue," her inquisitor warned, "or you will be in even more trouble than you are now. So, who are you?"

"I know you are after money," Amelia answered. "I am the Principessa Chiravalle. My husband's family are very wealthy and would pay whatever ransom you ask. But that might take some time. I think I know a way that you can fairly quickly get something of great monetary value, gold, that would be hard to trace once melted down. If you send this signet ring to my husband with your ransom note, it will identify me and he will respond. But do you want to know about the gold?"

"*Signora*, are you trying to trick us? Because that won't work," he said.

"No, I am serious," she insisted, "and if I tell you where the gold is, and you retrieve it, would you let me go, no questions asked?"

"Well," he answered, "I will need to discuss the idea with my bosses. For now, we will go for the ransom. Give me that ring."

Florence, the Next Day

Distressed by the terrible news of Amelia's kidnapping, Carlo Chiravalle opted not to go to his office, but to stay home in the Palazzo in case there was any news. Late the following morning, a young man on a *motorino*, dressed like a messenger service, stopped at the Lungarno gate and rang the bell. When the *portiere* opened the little viewing window to see who was there, he was handed a small package addressed to Carlo Chiravalle. The package was sent up to the *piano nobile*, where the prince was having lunch. He seized upon the package, knowing with dread that it was the ransom note and fearing that it would contain one of Amelia's fingers. He ripped it open, and found, to his relief, the signet ring and a letter demanding two hundred million lire in ransom. The letter outlined that instructions for payment would follow, and further that if Carlo should involve the Carabinieri, that Amelia would die immediately.

Meanwhile, in the remote warehouse, a high-up official of the Red Brigades came to interview Amelia. Although a bit weak, having only been fed stale *panini* and given water to drink, the princess was steeled to see what kind of bargain she could drive. "Tell us, *Signora*," he said, "what is this tale about gold?"

Amelia explained that during the war, an important shipment of gold had been hidden in the chapel at the family castle of Mariano in Umbria. While she did not know its exact location, she was sure that if they took her down there, she could get assistance from a staff member in locating the hiding place.

"Well," the man responded, "we are not taking you anywhere until your ransom is paid, but maybe we will check out the Umbria location."

6

MANHATTAN

Early March

Immediately after the exploratory expedition in the church at Mariano, locating the potential hiding place, Lucrezia telephoned Dickie at his apartment. It was seven thirty a.m. in New York.

"*Pronto*, Dickie," she began, "I think we have found the location where the gold may be hidden. It's down in the crypt. In three days, we return to Mariano with the mason who is bringing equipment to lift the paving stones. I'm not happy about the delay, but we had to provide the mason with written and notarized permission to begin work."

"Wow, that is so exciting. Do you think I should come over?" said Dickie.

"Yes, that probably would be a good idea," Lucrezia replied.

"Okay, I'll see about booking a flight, hopefully tonight,"

he answered. "Since it's the off season, the airlines don't have flights every day of the week. I'll keep you posted. Bye now."

As soon as Dickie disconnected, he dialed Alicia Milhaus at home and asked if he could meet with her first thing, as he had important news about the gold. Alicia said that was fine, she'd be there at nine sharp. On arrival at the Museum, he went straight to her office and explained what he had learned from Lucrezia and his plan for flying out that night.

Alicia listened, and when he was finished, she then spoke. "I think this is very promising news, Dickie, but maybe a trip just now is a bit hasty. I have not had a chance to update you on my meeting with our legal counsel, Bobby Satterthwaite, but he thinks our claim is somewhat shaky. We will need to provide evidence of several facts—one, that Philip Delancy died without a will; two, that his daughter and only heir is also dead; and three, that the 1939 letter of intent in our files is indeed binding—and that what we find is confirmed as the Delancy gold. I think that all this can be done, although it will, as all legal things do, require quite a bit of time. At the moment, there is no legal basis for us to claim the gold—maybe it would be a good idea for us to have a representative there, when and if the gold is found, so we could clearly indicate our presumptive ownership. That said, Dickie, you have my blessing to go. I would suggest you take a copy of the 1939 Flanigan and Caldwell letter, and also a copy of the 1909 Stuyvesant-Clinton catalogue, since it has full documentation of the gold and can be used to confirm what is found is indeed the same."

"That's a good idea," Dickie replied.

"In the meantime, I'll ask Bobby to be in touch with Interpol and find out how we might employ security to be there with us, if and when the gold is found. The gold's monetary value and its being so portable, combined with the remote and unprotected rural site, give me pause, especially since Italy is so ridden with terrorism."

Dickie raced back to his office and immediately dialed the Museum's travel agent. To his relief, it was one of the four days a week that TWA had nonstop service to Rome. He asked the agent to book him a business-class seat.

As the flight did not take off until eight-thirty in the evening, Dickie had the rest of the day before him, and a lot of nervous energy. He first called Lucrezia and told her of his arrival the next morning. As it was March, the di Florianos were, of course, in New York, and their Camerata house was closed for the winter. So he asked if he could stay at Crispiano.

Lucrezia immediately responded yes, and offered to send down a car to fetch him and bring him back to Umbria, which he gratefully accepted. He then asked his secretary to go to the department files and make a copy of the 1939 Flanigan and Caldwell letter, and also to check out a copy of the Stuyvesant-Clinton catalogue from the department library. Lastly, he asked her to book Tel Aviv Town Car for the trip from his apartment to JFK.

Just before noon, Alicia rang Dickie. "I spoke with Bobby about the security thing and Interpol. He has talked with Avvocato Marcello Porcelatti, his contact at Delano and

Pomeroy's corresponding law firm in Rome. Porcelatti told him that private security was not safe. The best route would be to work through Interpol to make an arrangement with the Carabinieri."

"I didn't know that," Dickie answered, "but if Bobby really thinks that's best, then let's go with it."

"I do." Alicia continued, "Bobby explained that the problem with private security firms is that they're riddled with corruption and are more likely than not to turn over the client's information to one of the terrorist groups, like the Red Brigades. Bobby also told me that Porcelatti offered to make the overture to Interpol, and he has accepted. Further, Porcelatti strongly warned that no action be taken at Mariano until the security can be set up." Alicia concluded, "It will probably take at least several days. I know you are eager to get going, but we need to take this safeguard. As soon as Porcelatti has any information, Bobby has asked him to be in touch with you at Crispiano."

"Thank you so much, Alicia, for your excellent help and support. I really appreciate it," Dickie replied. "If we can pull this off, what a great coup for the Museum."

"I agree," said Alicia, "but just be careful, please."

Although it was getting late in Umbria, Dickie phoned Lucrezia at Crispiano and explained the new development concerning security and the need to delay further work at Mariano until everything was in place.

"Oh," said Lucrezia, "Avvocato Porcelatti is an old friend of our family, and we have always had enormous respect for his advice. What he suggests make great sense. I will call Francesco Orsini in the morning and tell him that we must delay things for a few days. So I'll see you tomorrow, Dickie, no?"

"Yes," he replied. "I'm looking forward to being there with you. Bye now."

At the end of the workday, Dickie raced back to the apartment, threw some clothes into a suitcase, and caught his Tel Aviv Town Car ride out to the TWA terminal at JFK. After an easy check-in and boarding process, he was off to Rome.

Umbria, Early March

The day after Dickie's arrival at Crispiano, he received a phone call from Avvocato Porcelatti. The attorney, who spoke fluent English, told him that he had spoken with a friend who was a high official at the Rome office of Interpol. He had explained the situation briefly, not going into great detail, but indicating the need for a security force to guard the retrieval of valuable works of art at a remote rural site near Todi.

"My friend," Porcelatti continued, "said he would find out who would be the point person in the Rome Carabinieri office. That person could then steer you to the right official, not in Todi, but in Perugia, since it is the capital of Umbria." It was very important, the attorney explained to Dickie, that proper procedures and the chain of command be observed. If not, the entrenched bureaucracy would dig in their heels and create all sorts of delays. So, Rome would speak with Perugia, who then in turn would speak with Todi. Unfortunately, this process, and the reverse—back from Todi to Perugia and Perugia to Rome—would take time.

"In the interest of time, I took the liberty," the attorney said, "of giving my contact our approval to proceed."

Dickie expressed his appreciation to the attorney for his work in initiating the process, and told him he looked forward to hearing when there was any progress. *Well*, thought Dickie, *Alicia warned me about Italian bureaucracy, and now I see how right she was.*

He then found Lucrezia in the *salotto* and brought her up to date on his conversation with Porcelatti.

"Oh, Dickie," she responded, "I know how frustrating this is for you, but the *avvocato* is so right—we have to move methodically. Now, it won't do us any good to sit around here and be anxious about having to wait on moving forward. Last summer, you did not really have a chance to see Todi, so I think it would be fun to drive over, see the town, and have a good lunch. There is a little restaurant in *centro*, called 'Umbria.' Believe it or not, it has one star from Michelin. I'll ring Fabio there and book a table, okay?"

"What a nice idea," replied Dickie. "What time do you want to leave?"

"Let's go in about fifteen minutes," was the reply.

They embarked down the hill from Crispiano in Lucrezia's dark green Ford Escort Estate. Dickie soon learned that Lucrezia was an intrepid driver and seemed to have two speeds, stopped and breakneck forward. As they descended, the road entered a dark woods that obscured the view. Then, as they came out of the woods, Dickie suddenly saw, in the distance, the town of Todi, sitting atop a mountain. What was amazing was a large, central domed structure perched on the mountainside outside the walls of the town. It looked like it had been accidently dropped there by a helicopter.

"Good heavens," Dickie exclaimed, "what is that building?"

"Oh," Lucrezia answered, "that is the so-called Bramante. It is thought by many to have been designed by Donato Bramante, although it wasn't built until the early seventeenth century, long after Bramante's time. But never mind, it's wonderful, don't you think? It's properly called Santa Maria della Consolazione—isn't that a pretty name?"

The road into town ascended the hill and curved past the Bramante. The colored marbles of its walls gleamed in the bright sunlight. The steep road then passed ruins of medieval walls and led up to the top of the hill. They parked in the central *piazza*, which was bordered on three sides by crenulated medieval buildings. On the fourth side was the Duomo, whose façade was only half completed.

Lucrezia led Dickie back out of the *piazza*, past the opera house, and down to a small *piazza* that was bordered by a wide set of stairs leading up to a large church.

"This is San Fortunato," she explained as they went up the stairs. "It is much older than the Duomo and architecturally unusual, as its layout is in the Germanic Gothic hall style, where there are no side aisles."

Dickie was stunned by the brilliant whiteness of the plastered interior. After looking around the church, they then went down into the crypt to the tomb of the Franciscan poet and mystic Jacopone da Todi. "He is thought to have been the author of 'Stabat Mater,'" Lucrezia explained.

They departed via a small side street over to the Corso, which ran down the hill and through an ancient gate within the city wall. "This is Etruscan," she said. "The Roman and medieval gates are in later walls further down the hill."

They walked back up the Corso to the Piazza Garibaldi, next to the Palazzo dei Priori. Under the arches of the nearby Palazzo del Popolo, Lucrezia pointed out the fluted stumps of columns from the Roman era. From there, the cobbled street led down to the restaurant.

Dickie was having a wonderful time just being with this enchanting lady and hearing her musical voice as she explained the sights. *Oh, heavens,* he thought to himself, *am I falling in love?*

The restaurant, with its low, vaulted stone ceiling and huge fireplace, where food was cooking over glowing red embers, exuded an atmosphere of cozy welcome. The owner, Fabio Lucarelli, graciously greeted Lucrezia and then showed them to a nice little table for two near the fire. The warmth of the fire felt good after their walk in the brisk March air. Lunch, which began with a thick, hot, white bean soup, followed by grilled meats and vegetables, was delicious, and certainly up to Michelin standards. The red wine, *Rubesco Riserva* from Torgiano, was equally fine.

All in all, it was a very romantic interlude.

After lunch, they returned to Crispiano, and Dickie, who was still a bit jet-lagged and also a touch fuzzy from the wonderful red wine, excused himself and went for a nap.

Meanwhile, word of Amelia's kidnapping had reached Mariano. The news shocked Bruno Caparoli and made him feel guilty about his plan to bypass the *principessa*, and, only after the fact, inform her husband about opening the floor of the crypt in Sant' Ilario. So, he decided that he needed to call Florence. His call was taken by the *principe*'s secretary, who said that Principe Carlo was not taking any calls as he wanted to be instantly available should word come from the Red Brigades about further instructions. The secretary offered to take a message. Bruno, not wanting to be too specific with him, simply said that it pertained to permission for some urgent work that needed to be done in the chapel. The secretary told Bruno that the message would be passed on to the *principe*, and that he would call back with the response. The next morning, the secretary called back. He had spoken to the *principe* and conveyed the message. His response was that he was too upset by his wife's kidnapping to think about anything else, but as he trusted his steward's judgment, then it was fine by him to proceed with whatever work Caparoli deemed necessary.

Umbria, Several Days Later

Dickie was understandably anxious to have news from Avvocato Porcelatti. However, several days passed without another phone call. To divert him, Lucrezia arranged a day trip west toward Viterbo to visit the fantasy gardens at Bomarzo, and then the next day east, over to Roman ruins at Carsulae on the ancient Via Flaminia. Each day, her staff had fixed a marvelous picnic lunch. In spite of himself, Dickie, at least for the while, forgot all about the phone call and thoroughly enjoyed the excursions. It was wonderful to be with Lucrezia.

On the fourth day, Dickie and Lucrezia were having a mid-morning coffee in the *salotto* when Stefanella, the maid, came in and told the Marchesa that Dickie had a phone call.

Dickie hurried out into the corridor where the phone was located.

"*Pronto*," he said, "*sono* Signore Read."

"Good morning," said the voice on the other end in perfect English, "it's Marcello Porcelatti here. I have news. My friend at Interpol has put me in touch with the general in charge of the Carabinieri subdivisions—*generale di divisione*. We met in his office here in Rome, late yesterday afternoon. I explained that I represented an American client in a sensitive matter concerning the retrieval of valuable art in rural Umbria. I did not want yet to mention that it was your museum, because he very well could have asked if the Belle Arti were involved. We're not yet ready to deal with them. I also explained that, as the retrieval site was in a remote rural location, there was need for protection during the retrieval process, which was why I had turned to the Carabinieri. I asked the general to counsel me on how he would suggest proceeding. 'Before we go any further,' the general replied, 'could you possibly give me a little more detail? With some clarification, I will be better able to advise you. Like, what is the art, and where is it now?'"

"I was not really ready to get into those details so soon," Porcelatti continued, "but I saw the necessity of doing so in order to move forward. So, I told him, what we are dealing with is a group of eighteenth-century American gold hollowware that was hidden from the Germans during the war. We believe we have found the location at a castle in Umbria, and we also believe the rightful owners are Americans. If indeed we find the gold, we need protection during the process of retrieving it from the hiding place and then transporting it to a secure location, like the central Todi branch of Banco Monte dei Paschi di Siena. The general told me that this information was very helpful, and he thought this was a project for our Specialist Units Division, which, as their name suggests, deals with special policing activities including matters concerning works of art. He will be in touch with his subordinate who heads up that Division, explain briefly the issues, and ask him to be in touch with me. So," Porcelatti commented, "we at least have made the first step, and have the Carabinieri on board. As soon as I hear from the Director of the Specialist Units, I will meet with him and we will work together to map out the details of how to move forward. By the way, when it comes to the point when the Carabinieri are ready to come to

Todi to see the location and meet with you, I will come up from Rome to assist."

Three days later, late on a Friday afternoon, Avvocato Porcelatti rang Dickie at Crispiano and gave him an update. From Rome, he related, the *generale di divisione* had passed on the necessary information to the *generale di brigata* at the Perugia office. He in turn had contacted the *colonnello* in charge of the Todi area. "The Carabinieri are now ready for a reconnaissance meeting on site at Mariano," Porcelatti told Dickie. "In attendance for the Carabinieri will be a deputy of the Perugia *generale di brigata*, as well as the Todi *colonnello*. They expect that not only will I be there, but also the American client, and, as well, someone to represent the owner of the building in question. The *generale* indicated they had selected the morning of the following Friday for the meeting time. I told him," Porcelatti continued, "that would be fine by us. The *generale* ended the conversation by informing me that a formal letter of confirmation would be sent to my office."

"Well, that is great news indeed," said Dickie. "Thank you so very much for your negotiating all this. I will pass on the news to Lucrezia Atti. I think it is very important that she be a part of the meeting, as she is the liaison with the steward at Mariano, who also should be there, don't you think?"

"I agree," said the attorney. "I will drive up from Rome early next Friday morning."

Umbria, One Week Later

On a balmy late March morning, Lucrezia and Dickie drove over to Mariano for the reconnaissance meeting. As they parked below the castle, they found Avvocato Porcelatti, who had already arrived from Rome. The attorney was a tall, distinguished-looking, gray-haired gentleman wearing an impeccably tailored dark gray suit. Shortly thereafter, two black Alfa Romeo sedans bearing the Carabinieri livery pulled up with the representatives from Perugia and Todi. The Carabinieri got out of their cars and introduced themselves—Tenente Colonnello Giuseppe Bruni from the Perugia office, and Colonnello Franco Marini, who was the head of the Todi office.

The group walked up the street of the *borgo*, which led through the postern gate, and on to the Church of Sant' Ilario. The Mariano steward, Bruno Caparoli, met them at the church's door and then led the party inside. They proceeded up to the altar area and then down into the crypt. Caparoli had installed a strong portable light at the head of the Saint's tomb. "It is here, we think," he explained, as he pointed to the stone floor, "that the gold may be hidden." He then stomped his foot on the four squares immediately at the head of the tomb. This resulted in a dull but clearly hollow sound, which was in sharp contrast to the solid sound when he stomped outside the four squares.

"We want to lift these four stones and see what is there," Avvocato Porcelatti interjected. "What we expect to find is six carrying cases of varying size, which we believe contain the gold. Clearly, if that is correct, the treasure is highly portable, and we have asked you," he said, addressing the Carabinieri officers, "now that you see the situation, to give us a plan for securing the gold, both as it is exhumed and as it is transported to the bank in Todi."

The Todi official, turning to his Perugia counterpart, said, "Tenente Colonnello, do you mind if I answer?" After an affirmative nod from the other officer, Colonnello Marini began. "The first thing is that we need to keep this operation as secret as possible. I do not need to remind you of the dangers that lurk out there from terrorists. That said, as we live in a very porous society, we need to be prepared for any potential danger. It is our suggestion, therefore, that at the time the floor here is lifted, we have four enlisted men on station, armed with automatic weapons. We will position them at the head of the steps down to the crypt. When the gold is brought up, they will provide escort out to the entrance, where we will have an unmarked armored Ducato van waiting to transport the gold to Todi *centro*. The drivers of the van will also be armed. Once the van is out of the *borgo* and on the road, it will be accompanied by armed troops in two unmarked Carabinieri vehicles. The four armed men from here will travel inside the van to Todi *centro* to be on hand for the transfer from our van to the Banco Monte dei Paschi di Sienna in Todi's main square. In the meanwhile, we will be in touch with the bank manager and arrange for them to receive the shipment. One last thing, we request that all the names of those involved in, or aware of, the exhuming be sent to us for security vetting. Also, if you have their *coda fiscale* numbers, that would expedite things."

Avvocato Porcelatti replied, "We will do that. While I think we know everyone here well enough to be sure that there is no security risk, there are, in addition, Architetto Orsini and the mason, Enzo Sebastiano, and the archivist at the Palazzo in Florence. Marchesa, could you provide the Carabinieri with his name?"

"Yes," Lucrezia responded and then added, "There also is my aunt, Principessa Amelia Chiravalle, who knows of the possibility of the gold being hidden in the church, but she does not know that we have found the potential location. Most unfortunately, she was recently kidnapped by the Red Brigades. The family is still awaiting instructions about a ransom. Do you think that is something that might impact our project?"

"*O mio Dio!*" replied Marini. "That is terrible news but very important intelligence. It ups the possibility of danger incrementally. The lack of ransom news may indicate that she has told them about the gold being here, and that they are keeping quiet about a ransom as they want to keep the family focused on that, and lulled into a false sense of security about the gold as they scheme to retrieve it. This means we will need to be extra vigilant. Please send us the names today, if possible. I shall request that they be processed as a high priority, but it may take at least a week to ten days for our Rome office to respond. With that in mind, why don't we select Friday two weeks from now for the opening of the crypt?"

While not happy with the delay, all realized the prudence of the plan so were in accord with the date.

Florence, Late March

In a small warehouse located in another area of the same Florentine industrial zone where the kidnapped Amelia Chiravalle was hidden, the Red Brigades *capo* for the Florence area convened a strategy session. With the intelligence that Amelia had given her captors, the Brigades had contacted their compatriots in Todi.

Over the past ten days, disguised at various times as workers for UMBRA ACQUE, TELECOM, and ENEL, the Brigaders had staked out the Castello Mariano. They noted the arrival there of Architetto Orsini, and an older man, later identified as the mason, Sebastiano, as well as Lucrezia Atti, and noted that all had gone into the Church of Sant' Ilario, where they remained for nearly an hour. A number of days later, hidden in an UMBRA ACQUE van, the watchers' vigilance was rewarded. They noted the arrival of two uniformed officers in Carabinieri Alfa Romeos, and in addition, an older, well-dressed man in a Lancia LX sedan with Roman license plates, and lastly, Lucrezia Atti, who was accompanied by a tall blond unidentified man. They were able to ascertain, also through their local contacts, that this man was an American staying at Crispiano. And by tracing the license plate, they learned that the older man was an important Roman attorney. Again, the assembled group had gone into the church, where they remained for about thirty minutes. All of this suggested to the watching Brigaders that Amelia's intelligence was correct—that there was hidden gold, and that its location was somewhere in that church.

At his strategy session, the Florence *capo* laid out all this intelligence for an elite cadre of his lieutenants and foot soldiers. In the course of his presentation, one of his lieutenants inquired if the inclusion of the Carabinieri at Todi violated the terms of the woman's kidnapping and ransom. "Should she be executed?"

"No," was the response, "we may need her yet, and we also still stand to get big money from her husband."

After a few more details about what they had learned from the Todi surveillance, he concluded the briefing, noting that there was an urgent need to send a delegation down to Umbria to assist their Todi colleagues. "When the gold is taken out of the church, clearly with Carabinieri protection, the plan is to intercept it and take it to a safe location. There the heist will be evaluated, followed by division of the spoils with the Umbrian compatriots. Time is of the essence," he said. "I will personally lead the mission. We depart for Umbria as soon as this meeting is done. Are there any questions?"

7

UMBRIA

The Second Week of April

Dickie woke up at the crack of dawn. He was literally quivering with excitement. The previous two weeks of waiting for the fateful day, when they would go to Mariano for the exhumation, had been both an agony of suspense and a sheer delight. As a distraction, Lucrezia had taken him on various outings—Assisi, Arezzo, Gubbio, Montefalco, and Orvieto.

Perhaps the most memorable was the trip to Arezzo. It was the time of the monthly antiques fair, which Dickie found very interesting. But it was at the church of San Francesco when he saw the extraordinary Piero della Francesca fresco cycle, *The History of the Cross*, that Dickie experienced an amazing combination of awe and joy. His Piero "high" continued and then went up to another level when they drove on to San Sepulcro to see Piero's famous *Resurrection*.

Two days earlier, Avvocato Porcelatti had phoned from Rome to say that he had heard from the Carabinieri. All the names had cleared security. The date was now set for them to meet at Mariano at the end of the week, on Friday. As previously discussed, the Carabinieri would provide the security detail and transportation. Architetto Orsini would be there with the mason, Sebastiano, who, with Bruno Caparoli, would do the actual work of raising the floor stones. Porcelatti, of course, would be there, as would Dickie and Lucrezia.

After a light breakfast of coffee and toasted bread, Dickie and Lucrezia departed Crispiano in Lucrezia's green Ford Escort. Dickie brought his camera to document the exhumation, and also the Stuyvesant-Clinton catalogue. The drive over to Mariano took twenty minutes. On the way, they noticed an Iveco bucket truck with ENEL livery, servicing the powerline just down the way from the castle. They parked below and walked up through the *borgo* to the church. As promised, an unmarked Ducato van was parked by the entrance.

Inside, they were greeted by Colonnello Marini from the Todi Carabinieri office. "These men," he said, gesturing to four camo-clad soldiers armed with Beretta PM 52 submachine guns, "are our very finest. In addition to them, we have two men in the armor-plated van who are equipped with Beretta PX4 pistols. Down by the road are two armor-plated unmarked sedans, which will go with the van, one in front and one in back as it makes its way to Todi. Those drivers are also armed."

Just then, they were joined by Avvocato Porcelatti. The group made their way to the far end of the church and down the steps into the crypt. They had been preceded there by Bruno Caparoli, Francesco Orsini, and Enzo Sebastiano. Enzo and Bruno had set up floodlights and also rigged up a block and tackle to lift the stones once they had been pried up with Enzo's crowbars. The four Carabinieri soldiers remained above at the head of the steps that led down to the crypt.

"Well," said Orsini, "shall we begin?"

Enzo and Bruno began by chipping away at the mortar surrounding the four big paving stones that Enzo had earlier identified as being an anomaly from the mortar in the surrounding area. These four stones covered the spot that when tapped, had given out the hollow sound. Once the mortar was removed, the two men began to work with their crowbars to pry up the large square stones. Dickie could barely contain his excitement, and realized that, in fact, he was holding his breath. Once the stones were pried up, Enzo and Bruno turned them slightly to rest on the outside edges of the hole. Already, below, an open area could be seen. One by one, the stones were carefully secured with cables to the block and tackle and raised just enough to move them completely away from the hole.

The floodlights illuminated a small room, two meters deep and about two meters square. Resting on the stone floor were six dust-covered, rectangular objects of various sizes. Bruno lowered a small ladder, climbed down into the hole, and brushed off the dust. What was revealed were six dark brown leather-covered containers with carrying handles. They looked a lot like luggage.

"Oh, my God," shouted Dickie, "there they are!" He hurried down into the hole to take a closer look. He was astonished to see that each case was monogrammed with the letters "JSD" on the top. That was indeed a thrilling discovery as it further confirmed that they had found the cases James Delancy had made for his gold. While there was little remaining doubt that they had indeed discovered the Delancy gold, Dickie wanted to make one hundred percent sure, so he laid one case on its side and gingerly undid the closures. When he lifted the top, there he saw, nestled in a gray suede-lined interior, fitted to receive each individual piece, eight gold candlesticks with baluster-shaped stems set on octagonal bases. Dickie could hardly believe his eyes or the good fortune of the discovery. "We've found the Delancy gold!" he yelled up toward the opening above his head, to let everyone know the good news but also just to hear the words spoken out loud.

"*Per favore*, Signore Read," hissed Colonnello Martini, who was above in the crypt with the rest of the onlookers. "It is not safe to shout out that news. You never know who might be walking outside the door."

"Oh, sorry," mumbled Dickie.

He shot several photos with his camera, documenting the find, and then closed the carrying case. Turning to Bruno, he said, "Let's hoist these cases up to the crypt."

Enzo Sebastiano, standing at the edge of the opening, took hold of the cases one by one as they were lifted up by Bruno. Bruno and Dickie, who had scrambled up and out of the hiding hole, then loaded the cases on the *carrello* that

Enzo had brought to move his equipment. Flanked by two of the Carabinieri, they cautiously rolled the *carrello* toward the church door, where the other two Carabinieri were stationed. One of them used his *radiotelefono portatile*—a walkie talkie—to alert the men in the Ducato that they were ready to transfer the precious cargo. The van's sliding side door opened. Two armed men got out and stationed themselves at the front and rear of the van. Two of the men from the church began to transfer the cases down the three steps from the door and into the van. Dickie and Bruno stood by. Dickie was nearly in a trance, and was having trouble grasping the fact that the fabled and elusive gold was making its first step to the collection at the City Art Museum.

With the transfer complete, the four Carabinieri from the church joined their compatriots in the van. At that point, Dickie came out of his trance and announced that he wanted to travel in the van with the gold. "I am sorry, sir," barked Colonnello Martini, "but I forbid you to get into that van—it is far too dangerous!"

"Okay, I understand," Dickie reluctantly replied, as he stepped away from the vehicle and its sliding door slammed closed.

The two unmarked armored cars, waiting at the point where the *borgo* street exited onto the public road, were alerted by radio that the mission was on the move.

Earlier, as Lucrezia and Dickie neared Mariano, they had passed an ENEL bucket truck, which appeared to be servicing a power line about fifty meters from the entrance to the *borgo*. What they did not know was that it actually was in the hands of the Red Brigades. One of them, up in the bucket, had a clear view of the castle, the entrance to the Church of Sant' Ilario, and the parked Ducato. He also witnessed the arrival of those who were the exhumation party, and the four Carabinieri who earlier had entered the church. Lastly, he took note of the two sedans that were idling at the end of the *borgo* street. All this intelligence was relayed by radio to the Florentine *capo* who was stationed just out of sight, down the road toward Todi, in a parked Fiat 900 van that bore TELECOM's livery. It actually was a specially outfitted vehicle made for the Red Brigades. The van was protected by reinforced armored siding and had a souped-up Alfa Romeo racing car engine. Down the road in the opposite direction was another, similar sham van with UMBRA ACQUE livery. Like the first van, it contained six armed Red Brigade foot soldiers.

It was the plan that the bucket truck watcher would report to the *capo* when whatever it was, ostensibly the gold, was loaded into the Ducato and the van began to depart. The two sham vans would then speed to the *borgo* entrance, followed by the bucket truck, which would block the road to Todi. The two vans would stop side by side and block the road in the opposite direction, thus effectively hemming in the Carabinieri cavalcade.

When the watcher saw the Ducato start to roll, he sent out the alert. The two Fiat vans began to move. As the driver of the bucket truck had to lower its arm to retrieve the watcher, its move onto station, blocking the Todi road, was delayed by several minutes. The van with the Florentine *capo* sped past to take up its position at the end of the *borgo* road, where the other van was supposed to join up. However, just as the watcher had given the alert, before that team could start up their van, a huge Laverda harvesting combine, a machine used to cut and bale wheat or hay, pulled out from an adjacent field. The driver, unaware of the van behind him, turned toward Todi and the spot where the *borgo* street met the road. The width of the huge machine effectively blocked the road. The van driver frantically honked his horn, but the machine driver, used to the honking of irate motorists, paid him no mind and proceeded at his leisurely pace.

Just as the Ducato arrived at the end of the *borgo* street and was joined by the two waiting Carabinieri sedans, the fake ENEL bucket truck and TELECOM van were in place. While the other fake UMBRA ACQUE van was not able to get on station, the Laverda combine effectively did its job of blocking that part of the road. Immediately sizing up the situation, the Carabinieri commander radioed his troops to debark from their vehicles and take aim at the men and vehicles blocking their way. Simultaneously, the *capo* and five Brigaders, all of them armed to the teeth, sprang out of the TELECOM van. They were joined by the bucket truck driver and the watcher, each armed with a Beretta pistol. A fusillade from both sides ensued. The combine driver, fearing for his life, put his huge machine in reverse, and in his attempt to escape the scene, backed over the UMBRA ACQUE van. Although the sides of the van were heavily reinforced, the roof was not, and the van and the men inside were instantly crushed. Without the support from the second van, the Brigade force was reduced by six men, which gave the opposing Carabinieri valuable numerical superiority. The Carabinieri troops were hardened, professionally trained marksmen, while the young and relatively inexperienced Brigaders, although deeply committed to their cause, were rank amateurs.

In less than two minutes, it was all over. Six Brigaders, including the *capo*, were dead. The bucket truck driver was wounded—the watcher, uninjured. On the other side, one Carabinieri was dead, and another suffered a non-life-threatening injury. The combine driver, although badly frightened, was uninjured by the gunfire that had peppered his machine.

The watcher, a skinny youth of about sixteen, had dropped his pistol and put up his hands in surrender. "Don't shoot, don't shoot," he shouted. "I have valuable information about a kidnapping."

An armed Carabinieri foot soldier approached him, and ordered him to put his hands behind his back. He was then handcuffed. Colonnello Martini approached and said, "What sort of information do you have? If you are honest with us, the law may give you some consideration."

"There is an old lady," he replied, "who was kidnapped

and hidden in a warehouse in the *Zona Industria* up in Florence. She told my *capo* that there was gold hidden down here in this castle. After my *capo* made inquiries locally and set up surveillance of this place, he figured out that there really must be gold that you were going to remove. So, he made the plan to intercept your convoy and steal what you were moving. How were we to know that stupid farmer would mess everything up?"

"Well," said Martini, "you need to give us all the information you have about the location of this warehouse, and what security you Brigades have set up there. We can't question you here—we're going to take you into town for an interrogation."

The watcher was dispatched to Todi in one of the Carabinieri sedans. Two ambulances arrived to deal with the two wounded—one Carabinieri and one Brigader. Another ambulance was dispatched to take the body of the dead Carabinieri. The dead Brigaders were loaded into the back of a van. Once the bucket truck was moved out of the way, the Carabinieri convoy, with its precious cargo, proceeded on to the bank in Todi *centro*.

At the church, the remaining members of the exhumation party had been about to leave when they heard the fusillade of gunfire at the end of the street. They ducked back inside and Bruno Caparoli secured the stout wooden door. Ten minutes after the gunfire ceased, they heard a pounding on the door, and Colonnello Martini identifying himself. After Bruno let him in, he explained what had happened—the aborted attempt by the Red Brigades to snatch the gold, and the curious story told him by one of the survivors, of a kidnapped woman in Florence who had told the Brigaders about gold that was hidden here. "*O, mio Dio!*" exclaimed Lucrezia, "that must be my aunt, Amelia Chiravalle, who was kidnapped in early March."

Umbria, Later That Morning

Shaken by the Red Brigades attack, Dickie, along with the other members of the exhumation party, made their way out of the Church of Sant' Ilario and to their respective vehicles. Bruno Caparoli closed and locked the door behind them. Orsini and Sebastiano returned to Perugia. Avvocato Porcelatti suggested that he follow Lucrezia and Dickie back to Crispiano and discuss their next steps. They were in accord. The Escort and the Lancia set off in tandem back across the valley and up to the castle.

On arrival, the Marchesa, the curator, and the attorney settled down for a coffee in the *salotto*. Avvocato Porcelatti then put forth his suggestions. He thought it of vital importance that he go with Dickie to the bank and meet with the manager first thing in the afternoon. While he had, via letter and by a phone conversation, followed up on the initial contact made by the Carabinieri, who had requested that on their behalf, the Manager receive the cases for safekeeping, he had not had the opportunity to meet personally. The physical presence of Dickie was of the greatest psychological importance, he explained, in establishing the perception and hence precedence, that the Museum and Dickie, as its representative, were the rightful owners.

Meanwhile, the watcher, who had been bundled into a Carabinieri sedan, was taken down to their district headquarters, located below Todi, near the *Zona Industria* of Ponte Rio. There he was interrogated about the kidnapping of Amelia Chiravalle, the location of her incarceration, and the security set up there.

The young man was eager to spill, and gave the Carabinieri a detailed and clear description of not only the kidnapping, but also the warehouse location within the Florence *Zona Industria*. He further explained that the victim was under twenty-four-hour guard, but only one foot soldier was on station at a time. The guard was armed with a single Beretta pistol. This intelligence was forwarded to the Carabinieri office in Florence, along with the request that Principe Carlo Chiravalle be contacted and informed that the location of his wife had been found, and that a rescue mission was scheduled for that afternoon.

The caravan of the unmarked Carabinieri sedans and the Ducato van with the Delancy gold made its way into Todi *centro* and parked opposite the Banco Monte dei Paschi di

Siena. Prior to its arrival, local Carabinieri had blocked off vehicle access to the main square and also to the adjacent Piazza Garibaldi. Four armed foot soldiers secured the service entrance to the bank building. As the Ducato pulled up, the chief manager of the bank stepped out to greet their arrival. In short order, the six cases were transferred to bank personnel, the receipt papers signed, and the gold hustled inside.

A commercial wrecker was sent to Mariano to disentangle the huge Laverda combine and the remains of the mock UMBRA ACQUE van. At the same time, a Carabinieri van arrived to claim the bodies of those who had perished inside. This activity attracted quite a lot of attention among the citizens of the *borgo*, and word of that and the earlier shootout spread like wildfire throughout the *borgo* and then to neighboring villages and on to Todi. It was not long before the information was picked up, first by the local press and then by the national wire services. For the moment, the fact that a shipment of gold was central to the events remained unknown. However, the sudden closure of the two squares and the subsequent arrival of the Carabinieri caravan at the Banco Monte Paschi di Siena aroused considerable interest and speculation among the citizenry of Todi *centro*. It was not long before that facet of the story was also picked up by the press.

Umbria, That Afternoon

After the morning meeting at Crispiano, Avvocato Porcelatti phoned the manager at Banco Monte dei Paschi di Siena and requested an afternoon appointment as soon as the bank reopened following the lunchtime closing. Four p.m. was agreed upon.

The attorney and the curator made their way in the Lancia, down from Crispiano to Todi. After parking in the main square, they walked over to the bank, which was located in the ground floor of the Palazzo dei Priori, a crenelated medieval building dating from the early twelve hundreds. They entered into the banking lobby through the double airlock security door. This modern technology was in sharp contrast to the medieval stone vaulting of the lobby's ceiling. There they were greeted by a young man, secretary to the manager, who escorted them through the lobby and back to the office area. He told them that the manager would see them in a few minutes, and asked them to be seated.

Five minutes later, a tall silver-haired man emerged from the inner office. "Good afternoon," he said, "permit me to introduce myself—I am Paulo Montini, *Direttore Generale* of the Todi branch of Banco Monte dei Paschi di Siena. Please come into my office."

After they were seated, Avvocato Porcelatti introduced himself. "*Direttore*, we spoke on the phone several times. As I earlier told you, I am an attorney from Rome, who represents an American museum in the matter of important artworks hidden from the Nazis in 1944 and retrieved today from their wartime hiding place. May I introduce Signore Read, who is here to represent the American museum that is the rightful heir to the artworks."

Dickie understood that the attorney was purposefully vague in describing the "artworks" as he wanted to avoid the facts that they were gold and dated from the eighteenth century.

The manager, however, was not taken in by the attorney's vagueness. "I understand, from the Carabinieri, that what we have is six boxes of antique gold," he said flatly. "That being the case, I am obliged to inform both the Guardia Finanza, as it is gold and maybe stolen or illegal. I must also notify the Belle Arti, as it is antique and any disposition of it will require their determination and, if that is positive, issuing a permission. If I don't do so, I put myself and the bank in great difficulty, and in fact I have initiated a report to both agencies. I am sorry, but I must do my duty."

Dickie's heart fell. He immediately understood that weeks, maybe months or years stood between now and when the Museum might take possession of the Delancy gold. Even so, he whispered to Porcelatti, "Can they do this?"—to which the attorney whispered back, "I'm afraid so."

"Can I at least be allowed to see the other five cases, which we did not open at Mariano?" Dickie asked quietly.

"Let me ask," replied the attorney.

"*Direttore*," said the attorney, "we completely understand your position and the need to comply with regulations. However, I would like to request a favor. Would you be so kind as to permit Signore Read and me to open the cases and view the gold, to determine with certainty that what we have here is in fact the self-same American gold hollowware made in New York in the eighteenth century, brought to Italy in the early twentieth century, and bequeathed to Signore Read's museum? If it is not the same, then our work for the American museum no longer has purpose, and we will abandon the project."

"*Avvocato*," replied Montini, "your request makes sense, and by agreeing to it, I do not see that I am in conflict with my legal responsibilities to the Guardia Finanza or the Belle Arti. So, if we have no further business to discuss here, we can proceed down to our vault."

"*Bene*," replied the attorney, "I believe we are finished, at least for the moment, and ready to go with you to look at the gold."

"*Allora*," said Montini. "Permit me to instruct my secretary to make arrangements for the vault to be opened. That will take a few minutes. Would you like a coffee while we are waiting?"

Avvocato Porcelatti responded, "That is most gracious—yes, I would love one."

Dickie, who was impatient to at least see the rest of the gold, was not really sure he wanted to dilly dally over a coffee just then, but realizing that he had to be polite, indicated that he too would have one. Five minutes later, a little boy arrived with a tray of coffees from the café around the corner in the main square.

As is typical of most things in Italy, opening the vault took more time than originally indicated. Indeed, it was closer to half an hour before the secretary returned to inform the

Direttore that all arrangements were complete. In fairness, he had gone to the trouble to find and set up a folding table on which to place the unpacked items of gold.

The group made their way down a vaulted stone staircase to the lower level of the building. The chamber below was also vaulted stone. In sharp contrast to the surrounding medieval stonework was a huge, modern, reinforced-steel walk-in safe. Its door, two-and-a-half meters square, stood ajar. Next to it, one of the bank's security officers stood at attention. He politely saluted Montini, and simply stated his title, "*Direttore.*"

Dickie, Porcelatti, and Montini entered the space, where they found the six leather cases neatly arranged in a row on the stone floor.

"*Avvocato,*" said Dickie, "would you ask the *Direttore* if it is okay now for me to open the cases?"

On receiving affirmation from the banker, Dickie, his hands shaking, lifted the first case up to the table and undid the latches. Inside in the lower portion, he found the twelve dinner plates stowed in vertical padded slots, and within the upper portion, which also served as the lid, were the twenty-four tablespoons. He could hardly catch his breath, but he did gather himself together.

In planning for this moment, he had brought both his camera and the Stuyvesant-Clinton catalogue, which had grainy black-and-white photos of the Delancy gold. He quickly snapped a photo of the open case. The second case, somewhat smaller, contained the four sauceboats and ladles; the third, the tureen and ladle; the fourth much larger case held the salver and the two waiters; the fifth, the cake basket; and the last, the one opened at Mariano, contained the eight candlesticks. As expected, each piece bore the touchmarks DCF and N:York, and, as described in the eighteenth-century newspaper article, were engraved with the Delancy arms: a blue shield with three gold crescents.

Oh, my God, Dickie thought to himself, *the fabled lost Delancy gold has finally been found.* His elation, however, was dulled by the realization that there was a long road ahead before its acquisition by the Museum.

8

ITALY AND PARIS

April

In the days following the shootout at Mariano, the news took the nation by storm. First was the account of the aborted Red Brigades attempt in Umbria to hijack a valuable shipment, its contents not initially identified, and the superb performance by the Carabinieri in quashing the hijacking. Then came the story of the Red Brigades kidnapping of a wealthy Florentine Princess, the Carabinieri's storming of the warehouse in Florence where she was held hostage, and her successful rescue. That the Carabinieri's actions against the Red Brigades in both Florence and Umbria were carried out on the same day attracted the attention of the nation's press. And when the press figured out that the Umbrian castle where the shootout had occurred belonged to the husband of the kidnapped princess, the appetite to dig down into the details became insatiable. It took no time to discover that after the shootout, the Carabinieri had transferred something requiring high security from the castle to the Monte dei Paschi di Sienna bank in the center of nearby Todi. The story ran in the national press, such as Rome's *La Reppublica* and Milan's *Corriere della Sera*, as well as the more local press, like *Il Messaggero*, which circulated in Lazio and Umbria.

The story was also picked up by the Paris-based *International Herald Tribune*, but with a different slant. The paper had uncovered the fact that an American museum curator from New York was present at the Umbrian castle at the time of the shootout. The obvious question was why, and the logical conclusion was that he had some connection with the secure shipment that had been removed from the castle and transferred to the bank in Todi. The *Trib* writer working on the story used the byline "Ted Curtis." Gambling that the curator was from New York's City Art Museum, Curtis managed to get a list of the curatorial staff there. He then followed up with his contacts at both Pan Am and TWA, each of which had nonstop flights from JFK to Fumicino. His sleuthing paid off when he found a match in TWA's passenger manifests— Richard B. S. Read. Immigration forms indicated that Read was staying at Castello Crispiano, in Umbria.

Curtis's next step was to contact his close friend, Caroline Kuchler, longtime Paris correspondent for New York's weekly literary and humor magazine *The Knickerbocker*. Kuchler, Curtis knew, had a summer villa in the neighborhood of Crispiano. The intelligence he gained in a long phone conversation from Paris with Kuchler, who was in New York, was two-fold. First that the owner of Crispiano, Lucrezia Atti, was a niece of the owner of Mariano, where the shootout had taken place. Second, Kuchler related, she had met Read at a dinner party the previous summer at the villa of Arabella and Luca di Floriano near Camerata. At the dinner, Kuchler recalled, Read was very eager to find information about a girl assassinated by the Germans in Camerata during the war. She continued to say that Carter Bel Warner, also a guest at the dinner, offered to help him with an introduction to the local priest. What ensued, she said, she never heard, but suggested Curtis contact Warner. She mentioned in passing that Lucrezia Atti was also at the dinner.

Carter Bel Warner was known slightly by Curtis, as he had long been the Mediterranean correspondent for the weekly magazine *NewsAmerica*, which was owned by the same company as the *International Herald Tribune*. So, he took a gamble and dialed him directly. From Warner, Curtis learned that Read had indeed met with the local priest to learn about the girl assassinated by the Germans during the war. Having grown up in Italy, Curtis spoke fluent Italian. Taking another gamble, he placed a phone call to Padre Francesco Pianigianni in Camerata, and to his mild surprise actually reached him. From the priest, Curtis learned about Read's visit the previous summer, the lost American girl, and the letter from Flanigan and Caldwell with the reference to Adelaide van Wyck and her niece, Alexandra.

Edward Boylston Curtis, known as Ted, was the scion of a wealthy expatriate Boston family who had settled in

Venice in the late nineteenth century. While he had grown up primarily in Venice, his family circulated around Europe, where they mingled with titled Europeans and other wealthy Americans. Both the Curtises and Delancys summered at Antibes during the 1930s. It happened therefore that he knew exactly who both Adelaide Delancy van Wyck and her niece, Alexandra, were. He recalled that Adelaide was the sister of Philip Delancy and daughter of James Schuyler Delancy, famous for his angry exit from America and his horde of colonial gold hollowware. It was during the Antibes summers that the young Curtis had become friends with the Delancy daughter, Alexandra, who was exactly the same age as him. Ted now remembered that once, the young Alexandra had bragged that her godmother was a real-life princess. Then he also remembered, with some embarrassment, that his own mother had told him that his new friend, Alexandra Delancy, was part Jewish.

It was becoming clear to Curtis that, somehow, there was a connection between the lost girl Alexandra Delancy and the unidentified valuable shipment removed from the Umbrian castle, which was near the town where the Delancy girl had perished. Then it all suddenly came into focus. The part-Jewish American girl had been hidden from the Germans in rural Umbria, distant from Florence, where she lived. While the Delancys did not have property in Umbria, the Principe Chiravalle had multiple properties there, including the castle where the removal of the mysterious shipment and subsequent shootout had happened. Curtis recalled again how the young Alexandra had told him about her godmother being a real-life princess.

That's it, Curtis thought to himself. The godmother had arranged for the American girl to be sent for safekeeping in the area of Umbria, where her family had multiple properties. After the war, he remembered being told by his own parents that both Alexandra's parents had perished in concentration camps. They did not know what happened to Alexandra. They also told him that the legendary Delancy gold had totally disappeared, and it was assumed that it had been confiscated by the Germans and melted down. *But what if it wasn't*, Curtis thought to himself, *and the gold was entrusted by Philip Delancy to his daughter's godmother, Princess Chiravalle, at the same time as his daughter?* If that were the case, and the gold was hidden on a Chiravalle property, it stood to reason that the unidentified valuable shipment removed from Il Castello di Mariano, a Chiravalle property, could actually be the Delancy gold. The fact that the curator of metalwares at New York's City Art Museum was present at the Umbrian castle when the unidentified valuable shipment was recovered seemed to Curtis to provide virtually conclusive evidence that his theory was right.

Curtis met with his editor at the *Trib* and laid out his theory, explaining that he wanted to write an exposé on recent successful Carabinieri action against the Red Brigades, linking the aborted Umbrian heist of an unidentified valuable shipment and the release of a kidnapped Florentine princess whose family owned the Umbrian castle with his deduction that the mysterious shipment retrieved from the Umbrian castle was in fact the fabled Delancy family gold that had disappeared during the war.

His editor loved the idea and gave him carte blanche to proceed.

Curtis realized he needed to check on a few loose ends. One, proof the gold had actually been in Florence before the war, and two, the connection between the Chiravalles and the Delancys. He recalled that when he was about seven, his mother had been fascinated by an issue of the London lifestyle magazine *Country Life*, which featured their Antibes friend, Mrs. Delancy, in the frontispiece. Inside was an extensive article on the Delancy's Fiesole villa and garden. After some days of search, he managed to locate a copy of that issue. Sure enough, the frontispiece was a full-page portrait of the Hon. Mrs. Philip Delancy. The article, lavishly illustrated with both interior and garden photographs, mentioned not only Mrs. Delancy's parents, the Lord and Lady Greene, but also her husband's family, and referenced that the family's legendary gold hollowware was installed at the villa in a vault-like room. One of the illustrations depicted the Delancys having tea with their close friends, Prince and Princess Chiravalle. *Well*, thought Curtis to himself, *that pretty well nails it.*

The last part of the puzzle would be to get confirmation from the City Art Museum Curator, Richard Read, that the unidentified valuable shipment was, as Curtis deduced, the fabled Delancy gold. Toward that end, Curtis realized that a cold phone call would very likely not work. Rather, a face-to-face meeting would be required. But how to get entre? Then he recalled that his younger brother, Abbot Curtis, had been at Yale, about the same class as Read. A call to his brother confirmed that and also confirmed that he and Read had in fact been friends as they were in the same secret society—the name of which was not discussed. In the nearly twenty years following their graduation from Yale, the two had drifted apart, but Abbot was sure Dickie would be receptive to a call if Ted identified himself as his brother.

Through his contacts, Curtis was able to determine that Read was still in Umbria, staying outside Todi at Crispiano. He caught a late morning Air France flight to Fumicino, picked up an Avis rental car, and drove up to Todi, where he had booked a reservation in *centro* at the Hotel Cavour. The hotel was, ironically, just steps away from the Banco Monte dei Paschi di Sienna. After he got settled, he readied himself to place the call.

9

UMBRIA

April

After viewing the Delancy gold in the Monte dei Paschi di Siena vault, Dickie and Avvocato Porcelatti drove back to Crispiano. They met with Lucrezia in the *salone* for a glass of wine. Dickie confirmed the good news that they had indeed found all the Delancy gold, and also related the bad news— that the bank manager had conveyed its existence to both the Belle Arti and the Guardia Finanza and that he would retain custody of the gold until further instructions from each of them. Dickie was both discouraged and baffled about what to do next. However, his two Italian companions both felt strongly that the best defense against the two government agencies was to provide a strong chain of evidence that the gold now rightfully belonged to the City Art Museum.

"The problems the Museum's claim faces with the two government bureaucracies," Avvocato Porcelatti explained, "boil down to several key issues. For the Guardia Finanza, the question would be if the gold were contraband or in some other way was illegal, and the possibility that the Chiravalles, who might be deemed the current owners, had been hiding this asset from the tax authorities. It seems unlikely, in the face of issues with the Guardia Finanza, that Principe Chiravalle would lay claim to the gold, but that was something that would need to be settled. With the Belle Arti, as the gold dates from the eighteenth century, it clearly would need their approval for export even if all other questions about it, such as ownership, or it being an artistic asset vital to Italian cultural patrimony, had been satisfactorily settled. Proof of the Museum's claim would be of utmost importance in securing ultimate permission for export. The issue of opening the floor of Sant' Ilario without prior Belle Arti permission would be a problem for the Chiravalles, but not one that couldn't eventually be solved by their apologizing and paying a *condono*."

"We have some of the groundwork," the *avvocato* continued. "We have proof that the Delancy daughter perished in Camerata in March of 1944. Lucrezia has uncovered evidence in the Chiravalle archives that document the move of Alexandra Delancy from Florence to Umbria under Principessa Chiravalle's aegis. That is also documented by the local Camerata oral history. And it was information in the Chiravalle archives that led to the discovery of the Delancy gold at Mariano. We have to assume therefore that it was Philip Delancy's plan that both the gold and Alexandra be safely placed in the custody of his friend, Maria Pia Chiravalle. What we do not have is any indication of Philip Delancy's wishes via-á-vis the ultimate disposition of the gold, other than the late 1930s letter from his New York lawyers. That letter indicated that he wanted the Museum to receive the gold should he die without any heirs. So, it will be important to determine if he had any estate and if any heirs were identified after the war. It does seem strange that he did not have a will on file with his New York lawyers, but then, he seemed to feel safe in Florence and was still relatively young—early forties. And then with the war on and the later Nazi occupation of Florence, communication with New York may not have been possible. Finding some sort of written proof of Philip Delancy's wishes would be of utmost assistance to our quest, but the likelihood of finding such is very slim. So, we will have to move forward with what we have, Dickie." Avvocato Porcelatti continued, "Clearly a wealthy man like Philip Delancy must have had assets in America—stocks, real estate, etc. It seems to me that it would be a good idea if your director could speak with Mrs. van Wyck, who seems to be Delancy's nearest living relative, and find out, if that were so, what happened to them."

"That sounds like a plan," replied Dickie. "I'll call Alicia right away and ask her to contact Mrs. van Wyck."

One morning, as Lucrezia and Dickie were having breakfast, the maid, Stefanella, came in to announce that there was a phone call for Dickie.

"Did the caller say who he was?" asked Dickie, whose Italian had improved markedly during his weeks in Umbria.

"Yes," replied the maid, "he said his name was Ted Curtis, and that his brother Abbot Curtis was a friend of yours at college."

Oh, thought Dickie, *I remember Abbot—we had a lot of fun together. I wonder what he wants?* Then he suddenly recalled, *Of course, Ted is a reporter at the* Trib. *Why ever would he want to talk to me? But yes, I'll take the call.*

"Hello, Ted, this is Dickie here."

"Hello, Dickie, thank you for taking my call. I've been working on an assignment for the *Trib* dealing with the Carabinieri's recent heroic actions, and in the process, I came across the information that you were at the castle when the Red Brigades attempted to hijack an unidentified valuable shipment. It seemed to me that you might have some connection to that shipment, and since you are a curator of metalwares, I deduced that the shipment might be a precious metal. After making some calls, I learned you had been in Umbria last summer and became interested in the story of 'the lost girl,' who, I also discovered, was Alexandra Delancy. When I was a boy, my family summered at Antibes, as did the Delancys. We all became friends."

"What a remarkable coincidence," said Dickie.

"Yes, it is," answered Curtis. "Even as a boy, I heard about the fabled Delancy gold, and I am pretty sure that the unidentified valuable shipment is the Delancy gold. That in itself, if true, makes a far more interesting story than my original idea on the Carabinieri. I wondered if you would be willing to meet with me to discuss this further. I have found quite a bit of information on the Delancys and the Chiravalles. I assume the City Art Museum is making claim to the gold. What I know might be very helpful."

Well, thought Dickie, *this could be very interesting and maybe we will find some of the missing links. But talking to the press is always dodgy.* He decided he would tread carefully. "I would like very much to meet with you," Dickie said, "but I'll need to get clearance from my museum. I'll call them this afternoon, and get back to you later today or tomorrow morning when I have word, okay?"

"Okay," said Ted, sounding patient but perhaps a bit disappointed. "You can reach me at the Cavour in Todi. The number there is 885–2700."

10

UMBRIA AND NEW YORK

After Ted Curtis's call, Dickie waited until early afternoon—morning in New York—to place a call to his director.

"Oh, good morning, Dickie," said Alicia. "Do you have good news?"

"Well, yes, good and bad," he replied. "You may have read about it in the news but let me explain where we are." He related the tale of the exhumation, the confirmation that it indeed was the Delancy gold, and the frightening although abortive attempt by the Red Brigades to hijack it. He continued outlining the meeting with the bank manager and the bad news that both the Guardia Finanza and Belle Arti had been notified about the gold.

"Well, that's terribly disappointing," Alicia said when he had finished. "The involvement of these two Italian bureaucracies means it will be at least months, if not years, before the Museum might possibly be able to successfully realize its claim to the gold." Alicia also said she would immediately convey the news to Bobby Satterthwaite, the Museum's Legal Counsel, at Delano and Pomeroy, and ask him to start strategizing.

"Yes, indeed," Dickie said. "So I spoke with Avvocato Porcelatti and he suggested that finding the disposition of Philip Delancy's estate, if such happened, might lend credence to the Museum's claim."

Alicia agreed that a meeting with Adelaide van Wyck was the best place to start. "I think she may be out of town, but I'll try to phone her this morning," Alicia said, "and tell her the good news that the gold has indeed been found. I had not said anything to her before about your exploration and planned exhumation for fear of setting up false hopes. I'll also explain that we hope that the gold will pass to us and ask her about her brother's estate. She is such a reasonable person and a good friend to the Museum, so I do not think she will look askance at these very personal questions."

Dickie then mentioned the phone call from Ted Curtis and asked Alicia if she thought it a good idea to talk to him. "Well," replied Alicia, "the existence of the gold won't be a secret for much longer, and if his piece widely publicizes its discovery and our involvement in locating it, that might indeed be very helpful to our case."

"Okay," replied Dickie, "I'll call him after we finish and set up a meeting."

The next morning, Ted drove out to Crispiano, where he met Lucrezia and Dickie for coffee in the *salone*. Both sides exchanged all their information. Ted felt satisfied that he had all he needed for a dynamite story. Dickie felt confident that Ted would write his story in a vein favorable to the Museum's claim. After their meeting, they motored over to Mariano, where Lucrezia, Dickie, and Ted visited the Church of Sant' Ilario. There the journalist was walked through a reenactment of the discovery of the secret chamber under the crypt, and the later exhumation. They then walked outside and down the street of the *borgo*, where Dickie showed Ted the scene of the aborted hijacking and subsequent shootout.

Three Days Later

The weekend edition of the *International Herald Tribune* hit the newsstands all over Europe. The teaser on the front page was attention-grabbing. "Long-lost gold horde found in Italy: Red Brigades attack rebuffed: Kidnapped Italian princess released. See page 7." Inside, the Culture Section's banner headline read, "New York Museum Curator Finds Trove of Gold Hidden from the Nazis." The subhead read, "Hijacking by Red Brigades aborted. Kidnapped Italian princess freed." The byline read, "by Ted Curtis." The dateline was Todi, Italy.

"Two weeks ago," the article began, "after months of sleuthing by City Art Museum Curator Richard B. S. Read, his quest to find a long-lost trove of Colonial American hollowware, known as the 'Delancy Gold' and hidden from the Nazis during the late years of World War II, led to the identification of a castle near Todi in Umbria, Italy, as the potential place where it had been secreted. The location was narrowed down to a chapel within the castle, where the gold, long hidden in a secret chamber below the chapel's crypt, was successfully recovered. The recovery was conducted under the protection of a squad of Carabinieri, Italy's national police force. As the gold was being transferred from the castle, an Italian terrorist group known as the Red Brigades mounted an attempt to hijack the shipment. The attack was quickly repulsed by the Carabinieri troops and most of the attacking terrorists were killed. An earlier Brigades kidnapping of a Florentine princess, whose family owned the castle in question, had led to the Brigades intelligence of a possible treasure hidden in the Umbrian castle. That then led to their stakeout of the castle and the aborted attack on the Carabinieri convoy transporting the newly discovered gold to a bank in nearby Todi. A subsequent Carabinieri debriefing of a Brigades survivor of the shootout provided information that led to the rescue of the kidnapped princess. She has been identified as Amelia Chiravalle, wife of Prince Carlo Chiravalle, owner of the Umbrian castle Il Mariano, where the gold was recovered."

The article continued with the history of the gold and the

Delancy family from the eighteenth century, James's early twentieth-century departure from America in a fit of pique, his son Philip's marriage to a half-Jewish English heiress, and their ultimate death at the hands of the Nazis. It laid out the family friendship with the Chiravalle family and their involvement both in hiding the Delancy's daughter down in Umbria, and the concurrent hiding of the gold also in Umbria, and ended with the story of the daughter's, Alexandra's, tragic death also at the hands of the Nazis. The article's historic narrative concluded with the observation that it had long been the accepted consensus that in the course of the war, the Delancy gold had totally disappeared and was lost forever.

In the final part of the article, Curtis noted, "No one apparently thought more about the fate of the gold until, during a trip to Umbria last summer, Mr. Read stumbled across the tale of Alexandra Delancy's tragic death. Subsequently, on his return to New York, he learned more about the Delancy family and found out about the Delancy gold presumed lost since the war. That the fabled gold had been promised, years earlier, to the City Art Museum should Philip Delancy die without heirs, spurred Mr. Read to pursue contacts in Italy to determine if there was any evidence of its ultimate fate."

The article concluded, "It is Mr. Read's fondest hope that the Delancy gold will eventually enter the collection of his museum. Certainly, his heroic work in solving the wartime puzzle and rediscovering the gold lend considerable weight to that being the outcome. However, Read observed, there are a number of hurdles that must be cleared before that can become a reality. We sincerely hope his quest is successful. The City Art Museum is indeed deserving to fall heir to the Delancy gold."

The following week, the story was picked up by the *New York Times* and America's two weekly news magazines. Dickie's exploit and the rescued gold seized attention all over the country. The general sentiment, much to Dickie's pleasure, was that the Delancy gold should in fact end up in the City Art Museum.

New York and Umbria, One Week Later

Alicia Milhaus, at the City Art Museum, rang Dickie at Crispiano. "Good morning, Dickie," she opened. "It took me all this time to get an appointment with Mrs. van Wyck, as she's been out of town on a North Cape cruise. Yesterday afternoon, we had a very interesting meeting. As our conversation might include information valuable to our case, I asked for permission to tape it, and Mrs. van Wyck readily agreed. When I left her, it was too late to call, so I waited until first thing this morning."

"I appreciate that," said Dickie with a chuckle.

"I thought you would," said Alicia cheerfully. "Anyway, while still abroad, she had seen the newspaper accounts as well as the follow-up in weekly news magazines. She was very excited and indeed gratified that the gold had been found— and for our role in all of that. I explained that we hoped to be the recipient of the gold, but needed her assistance. I then asked her if she knew how the estate of her brother, Philip Delancy, was dispersed, if indeed there was one, as that would impact our case to inherit the gold.

"Here is Mrs. van Wyck's response—do you have a moment to listen to the recording?"

"Are you kidding?" said Dickie. "For that, I have all the time in the world."

Dickie heard the click of the recording begin and settled in to listen. "Well," began the voice of Mrs. van Wyck, with its cultured Upper East Side accent, "I probably should have told you this before, but as I am a very private person and loathe to discuss my personal affairs, and, since the gold was clearly lost, I opted not to go into any details when Dickie Read first began to ask me questions. Perhaps I was wrong, but at any rate, here is what happened. It was a complicated situation. At the end of the war, my brother perished in the Nazi camps, as did his wife, and in 1946 this information was confirmed for us by the State Department, as was the death in Umbria of my niece, Alexandra. And also, as far as we knew, Philip died intestate. I met with our lawyers at Flanigan and Caldwell and they advised me that as the next of kin, I would be the presumed heir. The estate turned out to be a large portfolio of stocks and municipal bonds that was managed for Philip, here in New York, by Morgan Guaranty's Trust Department. The arrangement was that Philip would cable them when he needed a transfer of funds. Morgan Guaranty would then cable the funds to his bank in Florence. After America entered the war the funds were sent first to Credit

Suisse in Zurich and then forwarded to the Florence branch of Monte dei Paschi di Siena. In the spring of 1944, when Philip's cables stopped coming, the bank began to hold the income in escrow until they had further notice. So, by late 1946, when we finally had the details about Philip's death, the accumulated funds had grown to quite a considerable sum. Philip's other asset was, of course, the villa in Fiesole. For that, we learned we would need to seek restitution from the current owners, who had bought the property when it was auctioned by the Nazis in the summer of 1944. As for the villa's contents, they had long disappeared as they were also auctioned at the same time as the villa. When I learned the amount of money accumulated and also the expected annual income, I was in a state of shock. It was enormous. I was comfortably wealthy with my own Delancy inheritance, and my husband much more so—we really did not need the money. And I felt guilty about becoming vulgarly rich just because my dear brother had been murdered. So, the lawyers at Flanigan and Caldwell suggested that I could waive my rights and, inheritance tax-wise, skip a generation in favor of our only child, James. As he was only seven at the time, Flanigan and Caldwell drew up a trust in his name, to be managed by Morgan Guaranty's Trust Department. The trust was set to expire when James reached the age of thirty.

"As a sort of closure to the dramatic wartime events, when the transfer to James was complete, I sent the family silver candlesticks to the village in Umbria. While we had no desire to own a property in Florence, the family villa was a valuable asset, so Flanigan and Caldwell, through their corresponding Italian law firm, initiated the restitution process. In typical Italian form, it took nearly twenty years before we regained title. The villa was then sold and the proceeds added to the James Schuyler Delancy van Wyck Trust.

"If it were up to me," she continued, "I would very much like for the City Art Museum to receive the gold. After all, were it not for Dickie Read's efforts, it would still be buried in Umbria. And everyone here in New York agrees with that writer for the *International Herald Tribune* that, by right if not by default, the gold should come to the Museum. But I'm afraid what all of this means is that I probably don't have a say, and despite public opinion, it will be up to James to decide, since he is the heir to the estate. As I just got home, I haven't had a chance to speak with him about all this. The bad news is that James is not a generous person. In fact, he has been profligate with his income since he gained control of it eleven years ago. He has been living lavishly and making disastrous investments in hairbrained schemes. And to top it off, he just went through a second, hugely expensive divorce. I'll talk to him and see if he might be able to see his way to letting the gold go."

Dickie heard a click on the other end of the line as Alicia stopped the recording.

"That was some useful information," Dickie said. "Thank you. At least now we know more precisely where we stand."

"We do. Also, as our meeting drew to a close," Alicia continued, "Mrs. van Wyck said that she would be in touch with

Avery Barton, her lawyer at Flanigan and Caldwell, to remind him that the Delancy gold was discovered by agents of the Museum. She also would ask if there were any questions of heirship, and additionally remind him of our 1930s letter from his firm. I agreed that we at the Museum would concurrently update Bobby Satterthwaite and ask for his guidance in light of the recent developments—discovery, Belle Arti, and our potential claim. So as soon as I get off the phone with you, I'll ring him and set up an appointment."

"Oh, my goodness," exclaimed Dickie, "what a saga! I am so glad Mrs. van Wyck is on our side. Hopefully, that will prove helpful. By the way," he continued, "I'm not sure what more I can accomplish here, so I probably should come home, don't you think?"

"That probably makes sense," Alicia replied, "but why don't you check with Avvocato Porcelatti and see what he advises? There is lots of work waiting for you here, but the gold is far more important, so as your director, I'm assigning the pursuit of the gold to you as your primary responsibility."

"Okay, got it," said Dickie. "I'll call tomorrow and let you know if I'm coming back or not. Bye now."

Umbria, One Day Later

After Dickie's phone call with his director, he spoke with Avvocato Porcelatti the following morning. In the course of their conversation, they agreed that there was not, at the moment, anything more that Dickie could accomplish in

Italy toward securing title to the Delancy gold. He realized, therefore, that he would have to bid *arrivederci* to Lucrezia and Crispiano and return to New York.

During the weeks that Dickie and Lucrezia had worked together toward the recovery of the Delancy gold, their relationship had slowly shifted from one of partnership in the quest to one that was definitely romantic. It was only natural, therefore, that on the evening after the recovery, Dickie and Lucrezia, on the high of their joint accomplishment, gave in to their physical attraction and for the first time made love. Dickie, needless to say, was ecstatic.

The morning after, Lucrezia, a devout Roman Catholic and, while separated from her husband, still married, seemed to have second thoughts. Seeming to recognize that Dickie was emotionally vulnerable, hurt by his recent divorce, Lucrezia delicately explained to him that while she did have strong feelings for him, her faith and her marriage precluded the relationship from really going anywhere permanent. If Dickie could live with that, she was, she told him, up for their simply being lovers.

While not happy about what Lucrezia was telling him, Dickie, ever the gentleman, responded, "Lucrezia, if that's the way you would like it, I accept your position and am happy to be your lover."

The several weeks that had ensued were idyllic. But now, it was time for it to come to an end. He phoned his secretary at the Museum and asked her to book a business class seat on TWA for the following day, and also arrange for airport pick up by Tel Aviv Town Car.

That evening, they had a lovely dinner together in Crispiano's grand vaulted dining chamber, followed by a long night of gentle lovemaking. The next morning, Dickie with great sadness said goodbye and departed for Fumicino via a Roman car service that came to pick him up.

He arrived at JFK that night.

11

ITALY

The Same Month

In the weeks that ensued after the Delancy gold's deposit at the Monte dei Paschi di Sienna in central Todi, the two Italian regulatory organizations—Guardia Finanza and Belle Arti—gave their initial response to the case. Their findings hinged one on the other.

Jointly they ruled that, as there was no evidence to the contrary, the gold, since it had been retrieved from a property belonging to Principe Carlo Chiravalle, was indeed Chiravalle's property. As such, the Guardia Finanza indicated that Chiravalle was liable for both the tax on this undeclared financial asset, and a penalty for its non-disclosure.

The Belle Arti stated that, first, Chiravalle would have to pay a fine for the unauthorized work in the Church of Sant' Ilario Chiravalle at Il Castello di Mariano. They further ruled that, as the eighteenth-century American-made gold hollowware was such a rare item, that it might fall into the category of *Patrimonio Culturale*. If that were determined to be so, the gold would then become subject to forfeiture to the Italian State, for placement in a to-be-determined Umbrian or Tuscan museum.

All this information was conveyed to the manager of the bank in Todi where the gold had been deposited. As Avvocato Porcelatti had been the link between the bank and the party that had discovered the gold, the bank manager passed these determinations on to him. At the same time, both the Guardia Finanza and Belle Arti communicated their positions to Principe Chiravalle in Florence. Needless to say, for different reasons, neither party was prepared to accept these findings without taking steps to legally protest them.

New York, the Concurrent Month

The day following her meeting with City Art Museum Director Alicia Milhaus, Adelaide van Wyke phoned her son, James, who was still in Boca Grande, Florida, even though it was nearly summer. She told him she had some very important family business to discuss, and wondered if he might come to New York to meet with her.

"Oh," James responded, "you must be talking about the Delancy gold. I read all about it in the *New York Times*. I was wondering when you would get around to calling me. I can't believe the gall of that *Trib* reporter suggesting that the gold should go to a museum. Since it was Uncle Philip's and since

I am his sole heir, as soon as I can get the gold out of Italy, it rightfully belongs to me. It's clearly worth a bundle and that'll come in very handy, as right now I am a bit strapped."

"James," his mother said, trying to be gentle and trying to stifle her annoyance, "there has not yet been a determination that the gold would go directly to you. After all, I am Philip's next of kin. It was only through my generosity that Philip's estate passed on to you. That determination will need to be made by the lawyers."

"Well, Mother," James snapped, "when the villa finally became a liquid asset that money came directly to me, so I don't see a difference here. In fact, I have already been in contact with John Burke, head of the Silver Department at Sotheby's, and also my silver dealer friend, Malcolm Ensko, and I can tell you there is great interest from both of them. I might get a better price from a sale at Sotheby's, but I would have to wait until the fall Americana Week. Ensko has a stinking rich and avaricious silver-collector client, a lady who lives in Los Angeles but is active with the antique folks at Yale. He thinks she might be up for buying the whole lot. If not, he would sell off the gold piece by piece, which is also what Sotheby's would do. Of course, I'd rather get my money all at once, but if the Los Angeles lady doesn't work out, I think I'll go with Sotheby's."

"By the way," James continued, "Ensko has done some basic spade work, and by making comparison with the weight of comparable eighteenth-century silver examples, found that just for the weight of the gold alone, at current gold prices,

I'm looking at more than two hundred thousand. So, the retail price should be somewhere in the millions. The sale will create quite a stir, I am sure."

"James, I beg you to not do anything rash. The sentiment all over New York is that the gold should go to the Museum. We are a very private family, and I deeply wish to avoid anything that would draw negative attention to either you or me. So please wait until we have more concrete information before you do anything more."

"Oh, Mother," James replied, "you are such an old fuddy-duddy. If you think you can avoid public attention over the matter, forget it. And forget any misguided notion that the gold won't come directly to me. I think this phone conversation is over!" With that, the connection was broken.

Following this very unsatisfactory conversation with her son James, Adelaide van Wyck placed a call to her personal attorney, Avery Barton, at Flanigan and Caldwell. They had earlier discussed the *New York Times* story about the recovery of the long-lost family gold. She recounted what James had told her and asked if there were any way he could be stopped from his planned course of action and sale of the Delancy gold once it was released for export from Italy, if that should happen.

"My dear Adelaide," Barton replied, "I'm afraid there is no legal course of action we can take to prevent the gold coming to James, as your brother's recognized heir. He is right. I'm sad to say, the direct flow of funds to him from the sale of the Florence villa does set a precedent. The only thing that would overrule that precedent would be if Philip had left a will, or specific indication of his desire vis-à-vis the placement of the gold after his death. Unfortunately, we do not have either one."

Florence, That Same Week

Principe Carlo Chiravalle could not have been more surprised that the Delancy gold was discovered at his Umbrian castle, Mariano. While initially annoyed that he had not been apprised of the exhumation project, he did have a trace memory that his steward, Bruno Caparoli, had tried to contact him about work at Mariano during the tense days after he learned that his wife, Amelia, had been kidnapped. He further focused on the fact that, were it not for the Red Brigades' abortive attempt to hijack the gold, and the intelligence gained after that, his wife would probably still be held hostage or worse, perhaps executed. So, he realized, he should not be cross with his niece, Lucrezia, for her part in the whole gold story. He remembered, as well, how close his parents were to the American Delancys, and that Philip Delancy had come to meet with his mother for several successive days before his arrest by the Nazis. When Carlo asked his mother what that was all about, she had told him not to ask, that it was private business between friends. He also remembered that it was about the same time that all the paintings in the Palazzo

Chiravalle picture gallery were taken down and disappeared, apparently to Mariano, where they were recovered after the war. Carlo realized now that the meetings must have been about the Delancy's daughter, his mother's goddaughter, and apparently the Delancy gold.

Now faced with a tax assessment from the Guardia Finanza that might add up to a considerable amount, Carlo wondered how he could disclaim ownership. As for the fine from the Belle Arti, he knew that he was stuck with that, although the amount could probably be negotiated. Toward the disclaimer of ownership, Carlo wondered if there might be as yet undiscovered information in his mother's archived papers. He made a note to speak to the archivist first thing the next morning.

12

FLORENCE

The Next Week

When Lucrezia Bianchini was young, and prior to her marriage to Il Marchese Piero Atti, she had become interested in antique porcelain and managed to get a job as an assistant to Florence's preeminent porcelain dealer. Ironically, he was not a Florentine, or even an Italian. Rather he was an American, Benjamin Moses, who had grown up in New York. Moses had studied at The Cooper Union in New York before he apprenticed with the prestigious ceramics dealers H. J. and B. Wilhelm, first at their 57th Street New York location and later in their London gallery. In the early 1960s, he moved to Florence and opened his own gallery, specializing in Italian, French, English, and German porcelain of the eighteenth century.

Over the years since she worked with him, Lucrezia and Moses had maintained a close friendship. So, it was not a surprise that she received a call at Crispiano from Moses in Florence.

"Good morning, Lucrezia," Moses began. "I understand you've been involved in some very exciting things of late. I loved reading all about them in the *Trib*."

"Definitely exciting," she replied, "but now there are all the problems with the authorities, so I worry that the gold might never leave Italy and go to the rightful owner, the City Art Museum."

"Well, it's because of your friendship with the curator there, that I am calling," Moses said. "As I think you know, I've been exploring the purchase of a small country house above Florence and near Fiesole. I found the perfect property and a highly recommended local *geometra* to help me with the purchase. The other day, I went to his studio in Fiesole for our first appointment. In his inner office, I caught sight of the most extraordinary Chippendale-style desk-and-bookcase, and it looked American to me. I asked the *geometra*, Mario Servilli, if he knew anything about the piece. He told me that during the war, there was an auction in Fiesole of confiscated furniture, and that his grandfather had, for a small price, bought the desk for use in his newly opened *geometra* studio, as the upper bookcase section made a perfect place to store his papers. And in fact, that is how it is still used. My dealer instinct perked up. I asked Servilli if he had ever thought of selling the desk, and he responded that in truth, it was not so convenient anymore, and he had in fact thought of getting a good modern storage cabinet. I have a strong feeling that the piece is American and

I think it might be a major acquisition for a museum. Which is why I am calling to suggest, if you think it a good idea, that you contact your friend about it. When I pulled out one of the candle slides, I noticed faint writing on it, but in the dim studio light, I was unable to decipher what it said. I took a couple of snapshots I can send you, if you like."

"Oh, Ben, that is interesting news," Lucrezia replied, "and I am sure my friend Dickie would like very much to know about the desk. So, send me the snaps, and I will be in touch with him."

New York, Three Weeks Later

After her conversation with Ben Moses, Lucrezia had phoned Dickie at the museum in New York and told him what she knew. She ended the call saying, "I'll send you the photos as soon as I receive them from Ben. In the meanwhile I send you many *bacis*."

"Can't wait," Dickie replied and smiled to himself. "Thanks so much for helping on a new project. It means we will still be talking. And *baci baci* back to you."

Intrigued, Dickie went down to speak with his director. Alicia agreed that an important American Chippendale case piece was potentially interesting news and certainly something to follow up on, depending on what they would find in the photographs. "I know the Moses Gallery by reputation, which is impeccable. So, if this turns out to be what we think it might be," Alicia said, "although Freddie Walton is our curator in charge of furniture, I think because of your existing relationship with the Italians, that you should become the Museum's point person to follow up on this lead, if what we find looks promising."

In the weeks following, Dickie met with his counterpart, Freddie, to discuss if there were any pointers he would suggest, beyond what Dickie had learned at Winterthur—to examine the desk-and-bookcase's overall exterior and to look carefully at the backboards and drawers to make sure the top and bottom had started out life together, and also to look inside the drawer fronts to see if the drawer pulls were original. Freddie, bald, but with pointed tufts of brown hair over his ears, wore dark horn-rimmed glasses and looked a bit like an owl.

"Look out for other inscriptions, beyond the one we know about, maybe on the back of a drawer—and look carefully, too," Freddie advised, "at the interior of the desk section. Try to pull out any part that might seem loose, and once something is pulled out look behind it for something else. Often in the eighteenth century, before the advent of banks, these desks had secret compartments, cleverly hidden and hard to find."

At last, after several weeks' wait—the *Poste Italiano* being notoriously slow—an envelope from Lucrezia was dropped on Dickie's desk. Impatiently, he tore it open. To his astonishment and delight, out fell three snapshots of an elegant desk-and-bookcase, the upper section crowned with a broken-scrolled pediment, flanking a tympanum richly ornamented with Rococo carving.

Dickie immediately rang Freddie and then, with the photographs in hand, raced over to his office.

Freddie took one look and gasped. "This is a fabulous New York example," he said. "I can tell because it's the dead ringer for one in that great Milwaukee private collection. Wow! Because of a disastrous fire in New York's most fashionable neighborhood—in the 1780s, I believe—New York Rococo furniture is extremely rare. The only difference I see is that while the Milwaukee bookcase section is fitted with looking-glass doors, this one has wooden, probably mahogany, panels instead."

The duo of curators met with their director later that morning.

"Alicia," Freddie said, "I think this is a very rare and highly important example of New York Rococo–style furniture, unlike anything we have in the collection here at the Museum. I would strongly recommend that the Museum pursue it and that Dickie go over and examine it for us. If you agree, I will lend him a blacklight so he can look at the inscription under ultraviolet florescence, which should make it much clearer, and also might reveal if there are any other inscriptions."

"That sounds like a plan," said Alicia. "So, Dickie, *buon viaggo* and *buon caccia.*"

"Yes," said Dickie, "the wishes for good hunting are especially appreciated. I wasn't able to snare the Delancy gold for our collection, and the prognosis looks rather dim. Perhaps, though, I can compensate for that miss, and through the contacts of my new Italian gold hunting cohort, deliver a superb New York Rococo–style case piece instead."

Alicia laughed. "That would be a win," she said.

"A win is a win," Dickie agree, glad to end the meeting on a positive note. "As soon as we're done here, I'll ring Lucrezia Atti and find out exactly where the piece is and how I can make arrangements to see it."

Umbria and New York, That Same Day

Mid-morning, Lucrezia Atti, at Crispiano, received a phone call from Ben Moses, who was in Florence. "*Pronto*, Lucrezia," he began, "you won't believe what I have done. I just couldn't resist the idea of buying the desk cheap and flipping it to my New York American antiques dealer friend, Isaac Frank. So, I asked my *geometra* how much a new cabinet would cost, and, after checking, he told me that one custom made to his specifications by a local *carpentiere* would cost him about two and a half million lire, which at the current exchange rate comes to a little over two thousand dollars. Obviously, he knew that I knew the desk was worth more than that, so I made him an offer of twelve million lire—that's about ten thousand dollars. He agreed immediately, which made me wince—maybe I was paying too much. Anyhow, I bought it on the spot. In addition to the photos I sent you, I also sent several to Isaac Frank, who rang from New York just now and said he was very interested but would have to come have a look-see. He said that if it turned out to be what he thought it was, it would easily fetch a retail price in the six figures. So, I'm calling to bring you up to date, to let you know that the desk is now in my shop here in Florence, and to say that if your museum friend is interested, he better come over very soon, because Frank plans to arrive here next week."

"Ben," Lucrezia responded, "thank you very much. I'll call my friend Dickie right away and, after we talk, I'll let you know what he decides."

Dickie had just returned to his office following his meeting with Alicia and Freddie when the phone rang. "It's the Marchesa Atti," said his secretary, as Dickie passed by her desk.

"Hello, Lucrezia," Dickie began. "This is an amazing coincidence—I was about to ring you about coming to see the desk. Can you advise me where it is and how I should make arrangements?"

"*Pronto*, Dickie," responded Lucrezia. "I just had a phone call from my friend Ben Moses. He told me that he had purchased the desk from the *geometra*, and that in addition to the snaps he sent you via me, he also has been in contact with an antiques dealer in New York named Frank."

"Oh," said Dickie, "I know exactly who that is—Isaac Frank. His shop on 57th Street is widely regarded as New York's finest source for American eighteenth-century furniture. And they also set the highest market prices. I'm afraid if we get into a bidding war with him, we will very likely be outclassed fairly early in the game. He has several private collector clients with deep pockets, one in Norfolk, Virginia, and the other in Houston. Well, anyhow, I'd best come over to see the desk. Where did you say it was?"

"It's in Ben's shop, which is located not too far from the Palazzo Chiravalle," replied Lucrezia.

"So, should I fly into Florence?" asked Dickie.

"No," she replied, "connections there from America are dreadful—you'd have to change planes several times. I suggest you fly to Rome. I'll send a car to bring you to Crispiano, and we can drive up to Florence the next morning."

"Okay, I'll try to catch the TWA flight out tonight. At any rate, I'll call back to let you know if I arrive tomorrow or the day after," said Dickie. "Once I do, could you please arrange with your friend Ben for an appointment to see the desk?"

"*Certo*," said Lucrezia. "I'll await your call. *Ciao* for now."

"Can't wait to see you. Til then, *baci*," said Dickie as he hung up.

Dickie's secretary made the usual arrangements—the Tel Aviv Town Car to JFK and a TWA business-class seat to Rome. Dickie rang Lucrezia to confirm, and late in the day he was once again off for Italy.

13

FLORENCE

Several Weeks Earlier

The morning following his resolve to find a way to disown the Delancy gold, Principe Carlo Chiravalle asked his secretary to summon the Palazzo archivist, Luigi Giovanelli. He explained to Giovanelli his goal of disproving ownership of the gold, and asked him to search through his mother's, Principessa Maria Pia's, papers to see if there was any further information beyond that which, Carlo understood, had led to the gold's discovery at Mariano. Giovanelli responded that, as the archives staff had been working with the *principessa's* papers in preparation for the paintings exhibition next spring, he was not optimistic about uncovering anything new, but he certainly would bend every effort.

So, when Giovanelli returned to his office, he was surprised that one of his researchers was there waiting for him.

"*Archivisto*," she blurted out breathlessly, "as I was looking through Principessa Maria Pia's personal copy of the 1944 paintings inventory, I found this strange letter interleafed between entries in the last part of the volume. I noticed that it was dated March 1944 and thought it might be about the transfer of the paintings, and hence pertinent to our forthcoming exhibit. I hastily scanned it, and found out it was about something else completely, which I do not entirely understand. So, I brought it immediately to you."

"Thank you, Letizia," Giovanelli responded. "Let's have a look."

Fiesole March 5, 1944

Dear Maria Pia and Filippo,

This is sent in haste as I have been commanded to report to the Gestapo Headquarters this afternoon, and I do not know what will happen.

First, I thank you from the bottom of my heart for allowing me to entrust my two treasures to you for safekeeping. Second, thank you for your help in getting that important document notarized. If anything should happen to me, it contains instructions for my estate and more importantly my intention for the future of my two treasures. I have hidden the document in my desk, you know where.

Forgive me for being so cryptic,
but we never know who else might
read this.

A presto
Philip

"Oh," said Giovanelli, "this is very interesting and comes at a most opportune time. The letter is obviously from Philip Delancy, and the two treasures he mentions are clearly his daughter, Alexandra, and the Delancy gold. The sensitive nature of the information and the concurrent perilous political situation would explain why the *principessa* secreted the letter in her copy of the paintings inventory, which was hidden at Mariano, along with the Palazzo's paintings, and recovered after the war at the same time as the paintings. I would guess that the *principessa*'s devastating cancer would explain why she did not say anything about the gold at the end of the war in 1945. The fact that the letter indicates that Delancy is not giving the 'treasures' to the Chiravalles, but rather entrusting them for safekeeping, is exactly the kind of proof the *principe* is seeking—that the recently discovered gold was not actually given to his family and thus is not legally his. We don't know what is meant by Delancy's reference to important documents or his desk, and that isn't really of interest, but the information about the gold is. I will let the *principe* know about it immediately."

Florence, Several Weeks Later

The day following Dickie's arrival from New York, he and Lucrezia motored up to Florence. On arrival, they entered the courtyard of the Palazzo Chiravalle through the Lungarno gate, parked the car, and then exited through the opposite side's gateway. They proceeded by foot along the cobbled streets to Ben Moses's porcelain gallery, which was on the nearby fashionable shopping street, Via Tornabuoni. The shop was located in a narrow, Renaissance-era building that had originally been a *farmacia*. The arched recesses along the lateral walls were intended originally for shelving and display of the ornamental *faenza* jars, containing the various drugs and spices. Those recesses Moses had updated with elegant, brushed steel members and glazing, where he then displayed his inventory of eighteenth-century porcelains.

Moses met them at the door. "*Buon giorno, cara* Lucrezia," he said as he kissed Lucrezia on both cheeks.

"*E buon giorno* to you, Ben," she replied. "Permit me to introduce my American friend, Dickie Read."

Dickie stepped forward and extended his hand. "I'm glad to meet you, Mr. Moses. Thank you for receiving us, and for letting me examine your desk."

"Please call me Ben," replied Moses, as they shook hands. "I have the desk in the rear in one of my storerooms, so why don't you come this way," said Moses as he gestured behind him. Lucrezia and Dickie followed him along the length of the shop and through a *pietra dura* framed doorway that led into the rear of the premises. They found themselves in a utilitarian space that had access from the street behind and served as a sort of loading dock for the gallery. Moses flipped on the lights, and there against the side wall was the desk-and-bookcase.

Dickie caught his breath. The case piece, standing about eight feet tall, was indeed impressive. He took note of the empty plinth between the scrolls of the pediment, where originally there would have been some sort of cartouche or finial. Freddie had told him that it was not at all unusual for these ornaments to be lost over the years. He took in the crisp quality of the Rococo carving on the tympanum as he ran his eyes down the façade of the bookcase section, over the slant top desk section and the drawers below. These were fitted out with what appeared to be fire-gilded drawer pulls with asymmetrical Rococo escutcheons.

Dickie, having taken an initial visual survey of the front, asked Ben if his assistants could pull the desk away from the wall so he could examine the back. Once that was done, he further asked that the lights be turned off so that he could take a look with the blacklight. That examination did not reveal anything amiss, so Dickie was ready to turn to the interior. He first turned to the four large drawers of the desk section, pulled out each, looking at their interiors, backs and bottoms, first with natural light and then with the black light. Again, there seemed to be nothing amiss, and indeed the hardware appeared to be the original. He then moved on to the bookcase section. Examination of the doors' rear sides suggested, under the black light, that the mahogany panels were probably replacements for the original looking-glass fenestration. The bookcase interior was fitted out on each side with eight large compartments in a two-over-two arrangement, flanking six smaller ones in the central section. The space was capped by twelve arched pigeon-holes. Three small serpentine-fronted drawers made up the base of the section. Examination of the section and the small drawers didn't reveal any new or negative information.

Next was the desk interior behind the slant top. At the base was a double bank of small drawers, also serpentine-fronted, which flanked a pair of vertical document drawers on either side of an arched prospect door. Above, also flanking the document drawers, were four arched pigeonholes similar to those in the bookcase section. Before he began further examination of this area, Dickie suddenly remembered that Moses had seen an inscription on one of the candle slides, and he asked him which one it was. Moses indicated that it was the one on the left, so Dickie pulled it out and turned on the blacklight.

To his amazement, the penciled script writing read "Delancy."

"Oh, my God," said Dickie, "since we know the *geometra* bought this piece at auction in Fiesole during the war, this must be part of the furniture confiscated from the Delancy villa." His heart began to pound with excitement.

I can't believe it, he thought. *I found the Delancy gold and now a Delancy family desk-and-bookcase. Of course, I couldn't have done it without Lucrezia's help*, he reminded himself. *It would be so great for the Museum if we could also acquire the desk.*

He hastily moved to the other candle slide and ran the blacklight over it, not really expecting anything, but just to be thorough. Again, to his amazement, there was another penciled inscription—"Henry Hardcastle" and "1769." Dickie had no idea who Hardcastle might be, but as the writing looked contemporaneous with that on the other candle slide, clearly it was something important, maybe the cabinetmaker.

He then reopened the slant top writing surface and started to examine the desk's interior. He pulled out all the small serpentine drawers, examining each for any further inscriptions, but only finding the numbers one through six penciled on their bottoms. Setting them aside, he pulled out the document drawers, peering inside to see if anything was hidden there. Next was the prospect door, which when opened revealed a stack of four small drawers, which he also pulled out. He noticed that they were not as deep as the serpentine drawers below, and wondered if there was a space behind them. But how to get to it? Remembering Freddie's instruction, that a whole section might be removable, Dickie pulled gently on the two flanking spaces where the document drawers had been. To his amazement, indeed the whole section moved forward to reveal a space behind. And, to his further amazement, he espied a thick, yellowed envelope.

With trembling hands, Dickie reached in and retrieved the unsealed envelope. He gently opened it, and pulled out a handwritten document that had what looked like postage stamps on the bottom and, under them, what looked like an official signature. The document, which was in Italian, began,

"*L'ultima volunta e testamonianze di* Philip Delancy . . ." At the bottom, above the stamps, Dickie recognized Philip Delancy's name, birth date, and what looked like information about a passport.

"Lucrezia," exclaimed Dickie, "is this what I think it is?" He handed the document to Lucrezia, who scanned it and then explained, "Yes, it is Philip Delancy's will, prepared and notarized on February 27, 1944. It is very simple. He leaves his estate to his daughter Alexandra Schuyler Delancy, but if she does not survive him, it names his sister Adelaide Schuyler Delancy van Wyck as his sole heir. A clause outlines two exceptions: his family's gold hollowware, known as the Delancy Gold, and his family's colonial secretary bookcase made by Henry Hardcastle. These two items the will leaves directly to the City Art Museum in New York. *Mio Dio*, Dickie, this is the evidence you needed for the gold, and the desk is just a dividend. This will be very helpful, too, for my uncle's issues with the Guardia Finanza and Belle Arti."

At this point, Ben Moses spoke up. "I am so excited for your museum, and for you, Dickie, to have this evidence about the gold. And it looks like I have a desk-and-bookcase that was stolen by the Nazis and, apparently, rightfully belongs to your museum. Instead of going through the painful process of restitution, I have a proposal. I have about twelve thousand invested in the desk, and if I had been able to sell it to Isaac Frank, I probably would have doubled that amount, either as a ten percent commission on his resale, or just a cash sale to him. So, Dickie, I am willing to offer the desk to your museum for twenty-four thousand, which for you is a bargain. What do you think?"

"I don't even need to check with my museum," the elated Dickie replied, "that price fits well into the parameters I was given when I set off on this project. So, we have a deal—let's shake on it." And at that point the two Americans shook hands, and Lucrezia gave each a big hug and a kiss.

EPILOGUE

Discovery of the Delancy will and the Delancy desk, as continuing parts of the lost gold saga, received wide press coverage both in Italy and elsewhere, with follow-up articles in the *International Herald Tribune* as well as US papers and news magazines. The implicit criticism of the Belle Arti's stand on the gold only served to harden that entity's resolve to hold on to the gold as part of Italy's cultural patrimony.

So, while the discovery of Philip Delancy's will was a major step toward Dickie and the City Art Museum taking possession of the fabled Delancy gold, for them, there were still issues that had to be resolved not only in Italy but also in New York.

On the Museum's behalf, Avvocato Porcelatti launched a legal campaign to appeal the Belle Arti's ruling that the gold was part of Italy's cultural patrimony.

In New York, the copy of Philip Delancy's will was turned over to Flanigan and Caldwell to initiate the process of probate. James van Wyck's vow to sue and invalidate the will in his favor was averted when his mother, Adelaide Delancy van Wyck, arranged a settlement with him that alleviated his precarious financial position and avoided family notoriety.

In Rome, Flavia Guiarducci, Director of the Villa Giulia, the museum of Greek, Etruscan, and Roman antiquities, saw an opportunity in the standoff between the Belle Arti and the City Art Museum. She made a clever proposition to the Italian Ministry of Culture, which oversaw the Belle Arti. The City Art Museum had recently acquired an enormously important red figure Greek vase, signed by both the potter and the painter. There was evidence that it had been looted from an Etruscan grave site at Settecamini, just outside Orvieto. The City Art Museum was resisting restitution. Guiarducci's idea involved a trade—the Greek vase for the American gold.

Negotiations between the Italian Ministry of Culture and the City Art Museum quickly resolved the double impasse, and the trade was approved by both parties. The Euxitheos vase, as it was known, was returned to Italy, to be exhibited at the Villa Giulia for ten years before transfer to Orvieto's Palazzo dell'Opera del Duomo.

The Delancy gold, and the Delancy desk-and-bookcase made by Henry Hardcastle, were installed together in the City Art Museum's Americana galleries in a vaulted space that replicated James Delancy's room at his villa in Fiesole.

That fall, the trustees of the City Art Museum, at a regular board meeting, passed a special resolution commending Dickie for his outstanding work in bringing these two important acquisitions to the collection, and further appointing him Chief Curator of the American Decorative Arts Department.

The Board passed a second resolution, expressing deep gratitude to La Marchesa Lucrezia Atti for her invaluable assistance in the quest to acquire those acquisitions, and named her a major benefactor of the Museum, which meant her name would be inscribed on the walls of the Museum's grand staircase.

Also, at the same board meeting it was announced that, in recognition of Dickie's rediscovery and rescue of the two Delancy family treasures, Adelaide Schuyler Delancy van Wyck had made a significant gift in his honor—the New York Queen Anne japanned high chest and matching dressing table.

Earlier, Carlo Chiravalle, relying on the recent discoveries—both Philip Delancy's 1944 letter to his mother, and the will hidden in the desk—was able to make a case to the Guardia Finanza that he was not the owner of the gold. The threatened penalty for hiding this asset and the fines associated with this misdemeanor were waived. As for the Belle Arti, he ended up only having to pay a fine for the unauthorized work in the Church of Sant' Ilario Chiravalle at Il Castello di Mariano.

At the same board meeting that recognized Dickie and Lucrezia, the Museum trustees, in gratitude to the Chiravalle family for safeguarding the Delancy gold, voted to send Principe Carlo Chiravalle an honorarium to cover the outlay of the Belle Arti fine, which had been incurred on the Museum's behalf.

At the end of the day, after the board meeting, Dickie went home to the apartment and settled down for a well-deserved Stoli on the rocks. *Well*, he said to himself, *who would have thought that a vacation in Umbria would have led to this adventure and for me the realization of an amazing curatorial quest? And meeting Lucrezia. My adored Lucrezia. There is no way I could have done any of this without her aid and support. Now that my gold quest is successfully accomplished, I think I need to turn my attentions to figuring out just how Lucrezia and I can work things out.*

ACKNOWLEDGMENTS

I would like to express thanks to my late wife, Janie C. Lee, for encouraging me to go forward with this story, which was originally written as a diversion during Covid. Thanks as well to my son, Will Warren, for his advice along the way. I also would like to thank Jane Kramer and Peter Sacks, who read the raw manuscript and gave me very positive feedback. Yoland Knull gave me the name of Greenleaf as a potential publisher, and in fact that came about. Lastly, I would like to express appreciation to my editorial team at Greenleaf for helping me make my Covid caper a published book.

ABOUT THE AUTHOR

DAVID B. WARREN is an expert on American decorative arts and the founding director emeritus of the Bayou Bend Collection and Gardens, the former home of philanthropist Ima Hogg that is now a museum of American decorative arts and paintings owned by The Museum of Fine Arts, Houston. He grew up in Wilmington, Delaware, and was educated at Princeton University and in the graduate program at the Winterthur Museum. Upon completion of the two-year Winterthur program, he moved to Houston, where he became the curator of Ima Hogg's extraordinary collection at Bayou Bend. He remained at Bayou Bend, later becoming its director, until his retirement 38 years later, when he was given the title of Founding Director Emeritus. He is the author of a number of books on both furniture and silver, and was a frequent contributor to *The Magazine Antiques.* He served two terms on the Advisory Council at Mount Vernon, and as a trustee and later an emeritus trustee of the Winterthur Museum, a position he holds today.

On a whim in 1979, Warren, recently divorced, accepted an invitation from Janie C. Lee to come for a visit at her summer home, an ancient house made of local fieldstone near the Umbrian village of Camerata di Todi. They fell madly in love during the visit and the next year were married. Lee first owned an art gallery in Houston and later one in New York, where she and Warren had a *pied a terre* in the Upper East Side. Together, they spent forty blissful and culturally stimulating summers at the Umbrian house.